LOSE YOUR BREATH

BOOKS BY D.K. HOOD

Don't Tell a Soul

Bring Me Flowers

Follow Me Home

The Crying Season

Where Angels Fear

Whisper in the Night

Break the Silence

Her Broken Wings

Her Shallow Grave

Promises in the Dark

Be Mine Forever

Cross My Heart

D.K. HOOD

LOSE YOUR BREATH

bookouture

Published by Bookouture in 2021

An imprint of Storyfire Ltd.
Carmelite House
50 Victoria Embankment
London EC4Y 0DZ

www.bookouture.com

ISBN: 978-1-80019-866-1
eBook ISBN: 978-1-80019-865-4

This is to all the people who go into battle for us on front lines everywhere. Thank you for your service.

INTRODUCTION

Black Rock Falls

Winter edged ever closer and there wasn't much time for Deputy Dave Kane to complete likely his last secret mission. A former special force's sniper, he'd worked his way up the ladder to become a protector of POTUS and part of the investigative side of the Secret Service. His life had changed dramatically the day he'd arrived in Black Rock Falls and met Sheriff Jenna Alton. He'd taken the position of deputy sheriff but, as an off-the-grid operative, POTUS could call him into active service at any time. But this wasn't the reason for his mission. He glanced at Shane Wolfe, and nodded. As the chopper lifted off, Kane adjusted his headset. He trusted the man in the pilot seat with his life and had done so for many years. Now they worked together, in Black Rock Falls, with a different life and future for both of them. Wolfe had been his handler during his years of service and when he'd asked him for this one last favor, he'd made the arrangements without question.

Kane's stomach clenched as the Potomac River came into view. He hadn't returned to Washington, DC, since heading out to Black Rock Falls. As the chopper landed on the roof of the local FBI building, he pulled on a baseball cap and climbed from the chopper. Wearing his sunglasses and with Wolfe close behind, he made his way to the basement parking lot and took the assigned vehicle. The slow drive to the cemetery gave Kane time to think back on his life with his beautiful wife, Annie. Circumstances had thrown them together and then torn them apart but he remembered every second…

CHAPTER ONE

Six Years Ago

US Embassy, Jerusalem, Israel

Darkness surrounded Annie Parkes as she made her way through the gates of the sandstone building and hustled along the sidewalk. The lighting dropped away to a few scattered lampposts as she hurried through the gates and headed along the narrow sidewalks. Deserted roads wound away in all directions, although as she walked, she noticed a few men congregating in store doorways. She hated this part of the day, walking along a dark road at night to where she'd parked her car. The winter moon cast long shadows that crossed the blacktop in zebra stripes and she quickened her pace. This part of Jerusalem was packed with dark side roads. The tiny place she shared with a friend didn't come close to the apartment overlooking the Potomac in Washington, DC, but she wouldn't be at the embassy forever. The job was for six months and she'd made it through the first half.

Hesitating before crossing the road to where she'd parked her old Toyota, she stared at the deepening shadows. Had she imagined the movement and slight scratch of shoes on the loose gravel, the click of metal? Unnerved, she grasped her car keys in one hand and searched the gloom with the light on her phone. She'd left her vehicle under a tree and she could hardly make it out in the dark. Overhead an owl shrieked and her nerves shattered as she ran to her vehicle. Fingers trembling, she pulled open the door and slid behind the wheel. Heart thumping, she locked the door and pushed the keys into the ignition. The instant she looked into the mirror terror gripped her. It was her worst nightmare. A man stared back at her from the back seat and the cold steel muzzle of a gun pressed into her temple. Terrified, she stared at him too frightened to flinch. Their eyes met and a cold chill slid down her spine.

"Drive." His face was covered but his dark brown eyes menaced her as he dug the gun into tender flesh. "Look at the road not me." His English was good but heavily accented with the local dialect.

Trying not to scream, Annie gripped the wheel white knuckled. "Where do you want me to go?"

"Drive toward Batei Nitin." He pressed the gun harder. "I will direct you. Do not make any sudden moves or I will shoot you."

Survival instinct setting in real fast, Annie swallowed the rising panic. *Keep him talking.* "Why are you taking me there?"

"Enough with your questions." He glared at her in the mirror. "Drive or die."

CHAPTER TWO

Syria

"Target moving into position. Countdown in three minutes."

The instruction was the last failsafe. Once the countdown began, they'd be no turning back.

"Copy." Ninety-eight H checked the instruments on his sniper rifle one last time and then relaxed. He looked at his spotter. "Get the hell out of Dodge."

"I'm gone." Ninety-eight G packed up his gear and vanished over the rooftops to the evac point.

Taking out a target was personal and he preferred to be alone. His rifle gave him all the information he needed and being six-five and two hundred and fifty pounds made him stick out like a sore thumb in this neck of the woods. He'd give Jimmy a better chance of escaping alone.

"Countdown in one minute."

There was no need to reply and he dropped into the zone. He hardly took a breath as his heart slowed and each blink felt like a minute. The dirty bomb-damaged room faded into obscurity. It would be just him and the target. Soon, the voice in his ear would count down the seconds. His eye dropped to the scope. Nothing but the flicker of a curtain at the open window and an empty chair came into view, but each day at this time, the target, selected as a threat to the free world, would sit at his desk and greet his visitors.

"In five, four, three, two, one."

Ninety-eight H squeezed the trigger, and the second the bullet left the muzzle he stripped down the rifle, packed it up, and headed out into the bright sunshine. He wouldn't see the aftermath. The target was over a mile away but as he made his way onto the roof of an apartment building, the confirmation came in his ear. He didn't need it. He never missed.

Gunshots echoed through the narrow streets; they were too damn close for comfort. He peered toward the evacuation point. A vehicle should be waiting to take them to the chopper but a militant force swarmed the area. Someone had betrayed them. He pressed his mic. "We have company."

"Abort evac. Repeat, abort evac."

"Copy." He needed to have Jimmy's six and pressed his com. "Ninety-eight G, do you copy?"

Nothing.

The group of militants yelled in celebration, shooting their weapons into the air. This meant only one thing. They'd caught Jimmy. He estimated his chances of taking out the twenty or so men as a possibility. No way would he leave Jimmy behind. Looking for a suitable place to set up his rifle, he glanced back over the edge of the building and swallowed in disgust. One of the militants held Jimmy's head high in triumph. He moved away from the edge and pressed into the shadows. The US would deny all knowledge of Jimmy's existence. He couldn't trust anyone and if he wanted to survive, he'd be doing it alone. The planned exit was compromised. He had no choice but to head in the opposite direction. After gauging the distance between his building and the next, he backed up to extend the distance and ran flat out toward the edge of the roof.

Heart in his mouth, he sailed out across the divide, misjudged the landing, and slammed into the side of the building. His fingertips grazed the edge of the roof and he hung suspended by one arm. Muscles burning with overexertion, he edged the other hand over the wall. Beneath his palms the crumbling edge of the damaged building shifted, his feet scrambled to find purchase on the top of a window frame. Bending his knees, he gave one almighty push and rolled over the edge onto a flat rooftop crammed with satellite dishes and air conditioners. Drawing his weapon, he stared around, but the damaged building was empty. The residents long gone, leaving their washing still hanging dusty on makeshift lines on the roof. Bullets rained down, striking the metal dishes and ricocheting in all directions. Shooting in the air was crazy. What goes up must come down.

Grabbing clothes from the washing line, he ran across the roof. The distance to the next building was an easy jump and he made the next six or more without a problem. He slid into the shadows of the next building, dragged the dark kaftan over his clothes and covered his head. Few Syrian men seemed to wear shades in winter but his would cover his blue eyes, and the deep suntan from long months in the desert would carry him through, but not his size. He needed transport and fast.

The door to the building stood ajar, propped open with a bucket. A woman pushed through carrying a basket of laundry. The second she slipped between a line of sheets, he moved with stealth, not making a sound across the roof, and headed down the stone steps into the building. The door to the first apartment was open and the sound of a child singing came from inside. He glanced into the dim hallway. In a dish on a table beside the door sat a set of keys. He snatched them up and headed down the hallway, slipping down the stairs and out into the late afternoon sun. He kept to the shadows, one hand pressing the fob, his gaze moving up and down the row of parked vehicles. Old sedans lined the road. He didn't recognize the make of any of them and glanced around him. The gunfire had stopped and engine noise rumbled through the streets. He dived behind a wall, pressing hard against the sandstone bricks as a convoy of militia, their black flag flying high on a battered military vehicle, drove past. He waited for the dust to settle and pressed the fob again. A battered silver Audi blinked at him. Wasting no time, he slid inside. The sedan smelled of dirty diapers but he dumped his backpack on the passenger seat and eased out onto the road in the opposite direction the militia had headed. He drove slowly, joining the line of traffic.

The instant the militia left, the town became alive again, people moving around and vehicles heading in all directions. He glanced at his fuel and heaved a sigh of relief. Unless he was stopped, he could go a long way on a full tank. Once on the outskirts of town, he'd need to avoid the military checkpoints, but without a map he'd be toast. The com in his ear and tracker embedded under his skin would give his location via a military satellite. He tapped his com for instructions. "Have you got eyes on me? I need a way out of this hellhole."

"Copy, Ninety-eight H. We're going out of range. Stand by."

Oh, that couldn't be good. If the plane carrying his command team had to bug out, they'd been picked up on enemy radar. He'd have to make it alone. "Dammit."

He waited, listening for instructions, but it wasn't the usual communications officer in his ear, it was his handler, code name Terabyte, who came through the earpiece. The connection was secure, something had happened to prevent his evac. He ground his teeth and waited for the bad news.

"Ninety-eight H, we need you north of Damascus."

He slammed a fist on the steering wheel. That was him, *Ninety-eight H,* no longer a person but a code name in an elite yet disposable team, and right now boots on the ground totaled one. His skill alone had kept him alive up until now but his odds of survival had dropped to zero. "Copy. Have you lost your mind? They beheaded Ninety-eight G and I'm next. I want an evac bird ASAP."

"General Parkes' daughter, Annie, has been kidnapped by rebel militia from outside the US Embassy in Israel. We know her location and I'm sending you to do an extraction. They're holding her in an old hotel. It's five hundred clicks from your current location. If extraction is impossible, you are ordered to terminate. Do you copy?"

"Yeah, I copy but I don't do mercy killing. I'll get her out, whatever the cost." Dragging a hand down his sweat-soaked face, he grit his teeth. "Is my team close by?"

"Negative on that. It's a no-fly zone, so get the package and make your way to Turkey. We'll evac from there. You know the deal: We don't negotiate with terrorists, so time is limited. Head north. I'll send you the coordinates and guide you around the checkpoints. You'll only be in communication with me. The line is secure. Move your ass, soldier."

"You're planning on sending me in alone to drag a young woman halfway across a hostile country without papers or money?" Ninety-eight H shook his head. "I'm a sniper. I kill people. I don't rescue privileged jackasses."

"You do now. Suck it up."

CHAPTER THREE

A cold wind blew through the boards covering the window, sending goosebumps over Annie's flesh. Inside the dim room, only thin shafts of sunlight illuminated the filthy floor surrounding the single chair the two bad-smelling men had tied her to. So thirsty that her tongue stuck to the roof of her mouth and with her head thumping in time to the beating of her heart, she stared around the room. Where the hell was she? The last thing she remembered was passing a sign to Hadassah-Helicopters Airfield. She'd driven to the gate and everything after that was blank. The embassy would know by now she'd gone missing. She'd called her roommate on leaving the embassy, same as she did every night, as a safety precaution, and by now her dad would know too. She tested the zip ties on her wrists for the hundredth time. They'd been tightened to cut deep into her flesh. Her hands had throbbed at first but had lost all feeling in the last couple of hours.

Shoulders burning from her arms being bound behind her at the elbows, she tried to hunch and relax to keep the blood flowing. She wiggled her toes. Had she been left to die? Maybe not. She could hear footsteps in the room above and she'd called out numerous times. The men she'd seen had been dressed in black but had remained silent, and yet as they'd left her, she'd heard a few words in Arabic. Terrified militant extremists had abducted her, she followed the instructions. She'd read about the chances of that happening and what to do percolated into her mind. Remaining calm and not giving them anything but her name seemed redundant as not a soul had spoken to her since the instruction to drive, all those hours ago. The usual people they grabbed in an attempt to arrange a prisoner exchange were of value to the USA, so why take her? A secretary working in the US Embassy wasn't much of a bargaining chip and she should have been safe in Israel.

If not to be traded, why else would they kidnap her? The idea of being sold into slavery hit her hard. Her stomach wretched and she tasted bile. At twenty-one, and petite, she'd pass for sixteen and with her natural blonde hair brushing her shoulders, she'd command a good price. Yet, surely if they planned to sell her, they'd at least feed her and allow her to use the bathroom to look presentable. If they had one in this flea-infested nightmare.

Sure her bladder would burst at any moment, she pressed her knees together. The occasional rush of water along a pipe running below the ceiling and disappearing through the wall made it worse. The pipe leaked, and watching the drips falling into to an expanding pool of water was torture. It had been hours since they'd left her alone. Cockroaches as big as mice had run across the floor in a whooshing sound, not one or two but enough to blacken the floor. They'd stopped and eyed her, feelers wiggling, and she'd jerked fiercely and screamed at them, making them run for the dark corners of the room.

Footsteps came from outside, the unmistakable sound of boots on tile. With her back to the door, she didn't see the men filter into the room but the stink of unwashed bodies preceded them. But it wasn't a man who moved into her field of vision. It was a woman, dressed in black with a burka covering her face. Only brown eyes rested on her. She stared at her. "Do you speak English?"

"You will not speak unless it is to answer my questions." The woman's heavily accented English was faultless. "You are an insult to women. I will allow you to bathe and dress in appropriate clothing.

You are not permitted to look at the men and they will not speak to you. Do you understand?"

Annie met her eyes. "Yes, but why am I here?"

The slap across the back of her head knocked her to the floor. She hit the stone slabs hard. Pain jarred through her temple and shot through her shoulder like a steel blade. The cold metal of a knife brushed her arms and wrists as someone cut the ties. Dragged to her feet, the metallic taste of blood coated her tongue and filled her mouth. A defiance her father had told her always to control rose up inside her. They obviously didn't plan to kill her—not yet anyway—and she'd fight for every last breath rather than cower to terrorists. She spat out the blood filling her mouth from biting her tongue, lifted her chin, and faced the woman again.

"Do you understand?" The woman glared at her.

Head spinning, as the need to defy the woman raged within her, Annie pressed her lips together and nodded. She had no choice. If she wanted to escape, she needed to survive.

"Follow me." The woman led the way from the room, through a maze of passages and into what resembled a hotel suite.

It was reasonably clean, with a bed and a bathroom, but like the small room she'd occupied before, the windows had been boarded up with old tin signs printed in Arabic. A single light bulb hung from a cord from the ceiling without a shade. On a wooden chair sat a pile of clothes. She stood in the middle of the room and scanned the walls. The expected camera sat high on one wall. So, they'd be watching her. A shiver went up her spine. Why did they want her? What was going to happen to her? She turned as the woman closed the door and stared at her.

"Bathe and dress. Then you will eat. Later we will explain what is expected of you." The woman indicated to the clothes on the chair. "Take these." She handed her a bottle of water from one of six on the table. "Do not drink the tap water."

The room with toilet, shower, and basin was in good condition apart from a rust stain in the sink. She dashed to the toilet and after drinking half a bottle of water, checked out every inch of the room for cameras and found none. They'd supplied her with a toothbrush, paste, shampoo, and soap. Thin towels hung on a rail beside the shower.

The small bathroom window was set high, but by standing on the toilet seat Annie could see the buildings around her. Many had been badly damaged. The streets below seemed empty apart from an army vehicle patrolling the streets. The latest information she'd heard about militants came from Syria. She swallowed hard. If so, there'd be no escape on her own. Terrified and trembling all over, she leaned against the wall, trying to think. She had no choice but to play along for as long as possible and see what happened. Her father, General Abraham Parkes, worked in the White House as an adviser. He'd have been notified the second she went missing. Acting submissive might give him enough time to arrange for her escape.

As she stripped, cold seeped into her bones. The chilled air made the injuries to her shoulder ache. Her fingers resembled thick red sausages and undoing buttons and zips was a nightmare of pain. The taps squeaked as she turned them but thankfully hot water poured out and she stepped underneath, washing as fast as possible. As she ran her hands over her face, she realized her earrings had gone missing as had the gold chain from around her neck. She stepped out of the shower and dried off quickly. After searching a small closet, she discovered a hair dryer, hairbrush, and some feminine products. It was obvious from the selection of items that her captors didn't consider deodorant, moisturizer, and hair removal essential.

She dried her hair and then checked out the pile of clothes. Thick undergarments to cover her from head to toe, a heavy black kaftan-style dress and a burka to complete the outfit. Obviously, the flat black boots she wore were suitable attire. She rinsed out her bra and panties and hung them to dry alongside the wet towels. Taking a deep breath, she stepped out into the bedroom expecting to find the woman waiting impatiently, but the room was empty and cold. Hunger gripped Annie's belly. Exhausted, she sat on the bed and stared at the door convinced her nightmare had just begun.

CHAPTER FOUR

Texas

After serving many tours of duty, in the most godforsaken countries in the world, Shane Wolfe had opted for a desk job in communications. He'd become the handler for three operatives, the voice they could trust implicitly to get them out of trouble. His charges, known only by their code names, often operated alone and they needed him, but right now his wife needed him more. As a fully qualified MD, he'd piloted a medevac chopper and saved many lives, but he couldn't save Angela. Her prognosis was terminal and he planned to spend as much time with her as possible. He had two options: He could hang up his shingle as an MD or he could use his expertise in IT as a computer nerd and sort out people's problems with their various devices. He had discussed his options with Angela and, as they had three daughters to care for, they'd decided he should work from home. There was a cellar under the house they'd converted into an entertainment area with access to the backyard. It would be perfect but he'd need to get over the next hurdle. After applying to leave on compassionate grounds, he stood in a waiting room for his commanding officer's decision. His mind drifted to the long sleepless night he'd spent communicating with Ninety-eight H in an attempt to keep his stubborn ass alive.

Ninety-eight H was the best he'd worked with. He'd lost track of the times he'd been dropped alone behind enemy lines, gotten the job done, and vanished like the mist. As a sniper, he never missed, and up to now, he'd protected his spotter. This guy was not only fearless, cold, and seemingly lacking in any human emotion but right now he was seriously pissed off. Yet the orders to send him to evacuate the daughter of a three-star had come from POTUS himself. The office door opened and the desk sergeant stepped out.

"You can go in now, sir."

Wolfe took a deep breath and walked into the office.

"At ease, Major. Take a seat." Major General Lukas leaned on his desk.

Wolfe sat down, back straight and eyes front. He had an inkling this wasn't going to go well.

"I understand the urgency of your request, Major, but we have a problem. Ninety-eight H doesn't trust anyone but you, and right now he's in the middle of a mission, which I'm sure you'll agree is complicated."

Wolfe narrowed his eyes. Was this a test? Missions were top secret and the life of the operative was at stake. One slip of the tongue and people died. "I have no comment on that, sir."

"We thought you might say that and as luck would have it POTUS is visiting Texas and has found a window in his schedule to speak with you." Lukas pushed to his feet. "Follow me."

Astonished, Wolfe followed Lukas through the familiar corridors and to a door flanked by two Secret Service agents. He pushed down the overwhelming gut-dropping experience of meeting his commander in chief and General Parkes. Heart pounding, he took the offered seat as Lukas left the room. Who was Ninety-eight H for POTUS to consider him above the other men under his command? Favoritism wasn't something he'd experienced and it gave him a very bad taste in his mouth.

"At ease, Major Wolfe. We're just three men chatting together discussing the future. I want to come to a suitable arrangement with you that suits everyone."

Dang, you can order me to kill the man beside you and I'd do it without hesitation, and you want to come to a suitable arrangement with me? What the hell is going on here? Wolfe swallowed hard and stared at him, stymied. He gave himself a mental shake. "Yes, sir."

"I know you're aware the package Ninety-eight H is collecting is Annie Parkes, General Parkes' only daughter, but you must understand why Ninety-eight H is so important to us." POTUS gave him a long considering look as if thinking before he spoke again. "I never show favoritism but there is a reason for my decision and this information can never leave this room." He paused a beat, his eyes fixed on Wolfe's face.

Why is that angry, robotic man so damn important to you? Wolfe swallowed the question hovering on his lips.

"During his time with us, Ninety-eight H has been involved in a number of highly sensitive missions, at most times initiated alone. He carries classified information that could destabilize the US." POTUS folded his hands on the desk and sighed. "Although we're confident, if captured, no amount of torture would make him talk, he also won't act unless he receives instructions from his handler. You, Major, are our only link to him."

Wolfe nodded. He knew about the missions but before he could say anything, POTUS held up his hand.

"We'll bring him home for a time when he completes this mission. As he's moved around during his career and spent some time in DC's Special Forces Investigation Command, he'd fit in anywhere and be safe here in the US, but I want him at the White House as part of my personal protection detail, although he'll be undertaking special assignments as required. It's not known, as nothing was released to the press, but he took a bullet for me at his father's funeral. Due to his exceptional vigilance, he noticed a muzzle flare and stepped in front of me without hesitation. I owe him my life and our country owes him a debt of gratitude. Therefore, you will remain as his handler for as long as necessary. I understand your tragic personal problems. My heart goes out to you and your wife but I will give you all the support you need now and going forward. We plan to set up your home as a communications depot to allow you to handle Ninety-eight H exclusively." He cleared his throat. "It's come to my attention that you're planning to continue your studies into forensic science, to become a medical examiner, I believe?"

Dumbfounded, Wolfe nodded. "Yes, sir, it was something I discussed with my wife as a career for when I left the service."

"Well, we'll make that a reality." POTUS opened his hands. "Any assistance you require, we'll supply for as long as you need. Your wife will receive the best medical care available; your kids will go to college. To everyone concerned, you'll be retired from active duty but you'll remain on the government payroll and will continue to receive orders and be in regular communication with my office. Be aware if the need arises, we might ask you to take another agent under your wing." He looked long and hard at Wolfe. "Questions?"

What could he possibly say? He shook his head. "No, sir." He cleared his throat. "When will I expect a team to arrive to make changes to my home?"

"I'm sure you've already discussed the alterations with your wife?" POTUS smiled at him. "The team will arrive about an hour after you get home." He stood and offered his hand. "Good luck, Major. Bring our people home. We have friendlies waiting for orders. Call into the command center for instructions. You've six hours before the next scheduled contact with Ninety-eight H. It's imperative you bring Annie home, whatever the cost."

CHAPTER FIVE

Syria

The temperature had dropped and the streets were emptying as people returned to their homes. Ninety-eight H moved in the shadows, keeping close to the wall. He'd left the Audi in a dark street and hoped it would still be there on his return. He needed supplies and stealing from people who had nothing wasn't his style, but he had other possibilities in the war-ravaged town. He'd spent his entire adult life observing in one way or another. He understood body language, the movement of people through a town. People who acted suspicious usually had something to hide. He'd noticed money changing hands. Drug trafficking happened on a major scale here and he had no problems stealing from criminals. The heavily armed men moved around in groups, shifting drugs, collecting money, but they all had a hub, a place to store both drugs and money. He just had to locate it without being seen. He hid in empty buildings, moving like a ghost, following, and watching. One mistake and they'd find him, torture him for days and drag him through the streets as a prize before taking his head, but they had no idea who lurked in the shadows. No way he'd ever go down easy, he'd be a nightmare they only saw coming once. The overconfident group he'd observed for the past few hours had led him straight to their lair. They'd arrived, collected bags, dropped off bags, and presumably left a small group of men inside.

Having the ability to move without a sound, was an advantage, killing without a sound another. He'd killed many men, in war and under orders, never in anger or spite. He didn't enjoy killing. In fact, he regretted taking a life but removing scumbags from existence was part of the job. He understood the difference between a psychopath and someone like him, that undefined person who could kill on command. He did have empathy and each time he took a life it meant something. Edging along the wall, he heard voices come on the cool night breeze, low, whispering, conspiratorial and the sound of a money-counting machine. The whirring noise stopping sporadically and the man giving the count. Being an Army brat had its advantages: He spoke six languages fluently and Arabic was one of them. He listened to the conversation. Only two men remained inside the small house. He slid inside the unlocked door. The hallway smelled of money and spices, as if the men had just eaten. His stomach growled. He hadn't eaten for hours. The sound caught the attention of one of the men, who hushed the other and lifted an automatic rifle and headed straight for him.

Pressing into a doorway covered by a curtain and hidden by shadows, he waited for the man to walk past. He struck like a snake, and before the man had time to take a breath, he covered his mouth with one hand and wrapped the other around his head. Applying one sharp twist, the man slumped against him, his neck broken. Not making a sound, he lifted the man into the room and lowered him into a chair by the fire with his back to the doorway. The other man called out to his friend in Arabic and then came out of the back room, grim-faced and waving his rifle in an arc. Ninety-eight H pressed his back to the wall and waited. His heartbeat dropped and all around him became calm, each movement of the approaching threat stretched out in slow motion. He breathed in and out and relaxed as if he had all the time in the world.

"Karam, what are you doing?" The man pushed back the curtain with his rifle and peered at his friend. "We don't have time to warm ourselves by the fire. The count must be done tonight."

As the man walked into the room, Ninety-eight H lashed out. One hard punch in the temple and he went down without a whimper, dead before he hit the floor. He dragged him into the room and sat him beside Karam and then went back to the doorway and listened, but the only sound was the wind brushing the house. He moved in silence, checking every nook and cranny for any possible hiding places and then slipped down the hallway into the kitchen. He had time. He estimated he had seven minutes before the patrol went past again.

A pot of food simmered on a stove and loaves of fresh bread waited on a bench, ready to be eaten. He grabbed a spoon, lifted the lid, and tasted the food to see if it was cooked. It tasted like chicken and vegetables in a thick sauce. He searched the small room; empty bags lay scattered across the floor. He selected a sturdy burlap shoulder bag with long handles and a zipper. He filled it with plastic bags of bills, neatly counted and wrapped, noting with surprise some of the packets contained US currency as well. He added two kilo bricks of heroin from a pile on a table and then pulled off his backpack. After, adding four loaves of bread and a couple of rounds of goats' cheese, he shrugged into the backpack and slid the burlap bag over one shoulder. His stomach rumbled as he eyed the hot food. He smiled, pushed a spoon into his pocket, grabbed a rag by the stove, lifted the pot, and hightailed it out the back door. As he pulled the squeaky door closed behind him, a militia truck rumbled past, slowing at the front of the house before continuing around the block.

Keeping to the shadows, he made his way back to his vehicle, slipping into doorways at any sound. Avoiding people on the street was easy, most seemed to be keeping well away from the gun-crazy lunatics on their patrol. The Audi was where he'd left it. It wasn't pretty, battered and rusty, so likely didn't draw any interest, but he'd wait and see. He slipped into the doorway of a ruined building and made himself comfortable. Using the scope, he searched all around, up and down, looking for the muzzle of a rifle or the slight movement of someone watching for his return. He waited but apart from the militia patrol rolling past like clockwork, no one appeared to have seen him and for sure no one had found the murdered men. He slipped across the dusty road and dropped his bags onto the seat, the pot of hot food fitting perfectly on the floor. He released the brake and the sedan rolled down the hill in silence. Before he reached the bottom, he started the engine and passed the corner of the street a few seconds before the militia truck went past.

He headed north, using his reliable sense of direction to get him out of the town. He cut his headlights the moment he turned onto a long dark road, pulled to one side, and dragged out a pair of night-vision goggles from his backpack. With luck, he'd make it miles before being spotted. In daylight it would be different. Alone out here, he'd be stopped by the militia, and his mission would be ended fast. He needed intel on the troop movements. He checked his watch. It would be hours before daylight and hunger gnawed at his gut. He'd driven five miles or so before spotting a bomb-damaged building. The car bumped off the road as he weaved through debris and parked inside the broken shell. He took a long deep breath and checked his surroundings. He'd be safe for a while and have long enough to fill his empty stomach. He pulled the pot onto his lap and pulled out the spoon—well, ladle would be a better description—and tucked in. After a few mouthfuls, he hit his com. "Terabyte, do you copy?"

He waited, repeating the message a few times. The sky was clear and the moon surrounded by a million stars. It was a small piece of normality in his tumultuous world. He'd often stare at the moon while stateside, and at times of deep conflict, he wished he could be way out west, maybe in Big Sky Country, hunting, fishing, and miles away from any hostiles. Maybe one day he'd go way off the grid and find him some peace. He'd get a dog and find a cozy little diner that sold the world's best peach pie. He'd given up the idea of marriage, kids, and a white picket fence the moment he'd finished military training and picked up a sniper rifle. He'd known what his life would be like. He'd never inflict the insecurity on someone he loved. It had been different for his dad, a two-star general on the way up. He'd moved around the world, taking his family with him. He'd enjoyed his childhood, growing up with his baby sister, but the day the men in dress uniform arrived to inform them his father had taken a bullet, he'd witnessed firsthand how his mom had suffered. She'd given up on life and died a month later. He pressed his com again. "Terabyte, do you copy?"

*"How are things in Vegas?"*Terabyte cleared his throat. *"Damn cold at this time of the year, I hear. Win any money at the casino?"*

"Copy that. Man, I hit paydirt." Ninety-eight H took another scoop of stew or whatever and chewed slowly. "But let's cut the crap." He drank from his canteen. "I need you to guide me out of here. Where do I pick up the package?"

"Here lies the problem."

CHAPTER SIX

Too terrified to close her eyes, Annie had huddled on the bed all night. The noise of boots on the floor outside her room made her tremble but she refused to cry. They'd taken photographs of her and she could hear men arguing long and loud into the night. As the first rays of sunlight pierced the boards across the window, she heard the key in the lock turning. The woman from before walked in and stared at her, shaking her head.

"You've slept in your clothes. I thought you would. You have no sense at all." She placed a tray of food on the chair, dropped a pile of fresh clothes onto the bed, and glared at her. "The mighty general you call father has abandoned you. Our leader wanted to behead you to show everyone how much we despise all America stands for but he had a better idea—a bigger insult. We are selling you to the highest bidder." She backed out of the room. "Make sure you don't smell. We have bidders arriving soon."

Dry-retching, Annie ran for the bathroom. Head throbbing, she hung over the filthy toilet but only bile filled her mouth. She straightened, undressed, showered, and brushed her hair. A tremble shivered over her. She didn't want to even imagine what it would be like being a sex slave. Swallowing her fear, she walked back into the bedroom, dressed, and collected the tray. She had to think. Escaping from her current prison would be impossible but there may be a slim chance from a brothel or wherever they'd take her. Surely if someone purchased her, she'd have some value to them. They may in time give her a modicum of freedom. She'd need to keep up her strength and she ate the fresh bread and cheese. She craved coffee but water would have to do, although the smell of coffee had drifted through the door. Obviously, it had been brewed for the men.

It seemed like forever before the door opened again. The woman walked in flanked by two men. One of them tied a rough rope around her wrists and led her like a dog through passageways and down steps into a hall of some kind. The noise in the room sounded like a flock of geese, and no wonder, from the groups of men waiting inside. The room was in reasonably good shape, the windows intact, and from the tables and chairs along one wall had at one time been a function room in the hotel. The heavily armed men fell silent as she walked in. It was obvious who were the prospective buyers from the way the armed men surrounded a central figure in each group.

Pulled by the rope, Annie stumbled behind the man dragging her to stand before each of the seated men. They all looked at her, not that they could see much with only her eyes visible from the gap in the burka. After they'd paraded her and the man dragging her had argued with them like a barking pack of wolves, the money came out, or other items including gold jewelry and coins. It seemed the daughter of an American general was in high demand. She trembled at the thought of what they'd do to her and kept her eyes on the floor. Making eye contact would be a definite insult to these men. She heard loud voices and the man pulling her stopped. Someone of importance had come into the hall. She chanced a glance at a tall man in robes surrounded by heavily armed militia. The man spoke fast and within seconds, another man ran forward and produced a chair for him, followed by a small cup without handles of something that smelled like coffee. The important visitor waved a hand beckoning her forward and leaned back, looking at her, but she couldn't see his eyes behind the sunglasses. He sipped the drink and made a comment, his mouth spreading into a wide grin. The next moment someone pushed her and she stumbled closer. When one of the other men produced a stack of US bills and placed them on a table with a confident smile, the tall man shook his head and snorted in amusement and then waved one of his men forward. The man dropped a brick of something, probably drugs, wrapped in plastic onto the table and then took hold of her rope. The bartering was over. No one argued. Had a drug lord purchased her? The tall man finished his drink and stood. Annie gaped at the back of him as he walked from the room. In all her time in the Middle East she'd never seen a man that size.

Dragged out into the sunshine, she followed the man toward an old limousine, bearing flags on the hood. Whoever this man was, he must be someone of high standing. Once outside, the big man turned to look at her. He didn't say a word as he untied her, tossed her over one broad shoulder, and carried her to the limousine. He opened the door, dropped her to her feet and pushed her into the vehicle. As she fell onto the seat, and he sat beside her, the vehicle took off at full speed in a convoy of four old cars. Heart thumping, Annie kept her head down, too scared to move. The man beside her was conversing with the driver in Arabic and after about an hour they drove into a small town and pulled up outside a house. The door opened and a man beckoned her out. Armed men surrounded her as they ushered her through the front door and pushed her into a room with a table and chairs and a stove of sorts. The home smelled of spices, coffee, and bread. Surely this dump couldn't belong to the man with the limousine. It was barely a lean-to. One of the men dragged the burka off her head, took a photograph of her with his phone, and left her alone with the tall man. Petrified, she stared at her feet as the door closed behind him.

"You sure don't say much, Annie." The American accent caught her by surprise. "I figured you'd be screaming and trying to scratch out my eyes by now."

Anger running out of control at his arrogance, Annie turned and looked at the man. "Traitor! Drug trafficker! I hope you die real slow when they catch you, and they will. My dad won't leave me here. He'll hunt you down."

The man removed his sunglasses to reveal dark blue eyes. His teeth flashed white as he grinned. "Your dad must be a close friend of POTUS to send me to get your ass out of trouble. What were you thinking, wandering around the backstreets of Israel at night on your lonesome?"

She wanted to slap the silly grin off his face. "I'm twenty-one and I work for the US Embassy. I don't need your permission or anyone else's to do as I please."

"Twenty-one, huh?" He studied her more closely. "FYI, you're not going back to the embassy." He pulled out a chair for her. "Sit down, we aren't out of this yet. I don't have a team and we'll have to rely on a few friendlies. It's going to be tough going. Are you tough enough, Annie?"

Lifting her chin, she glared at him. From his expression he considered her a burden, too weak to survive, but she'd done fine so far. "Can I keep up with you? Sure, I can. I'm tougher than I look." She gripped the arms of the chair. "I can use a weapon. My dad took me out to the practice range regularly and taught me self-defense."

"We're gonna need more than self-defense to make it out of here. I'm the only weapon you need, but people will die and I can't have you screaming or fainting every time you see blood. It's going to be nasty. Depending what happens between now and then, we might have to find our own way back to the States." He placed a small cup without handles in front of her and filled it from a pot and then pushed the plate on the table, filled with bread, dates, and cheese toward her. "Eat. We need to keep moving. It's only a matter of time before they discover the guy I impersonated is dead."

Annie sniffed the yellowish spicy drink. It smelled like coffee. The strange brew was sweet and rich with spices. "I won't faint or scream. I just want to make it out of here alive."

"Well, I'll do my best but you must do as I say." He narrowed his gaze at her. "A mistake, a split-second hesitation could cost us our lives." He waved a hand as if encompassing their surroundings. "Best you don't think, just follow orders. Keeping you safe is my priority. You'll just have to trust me."

"Okay." She watched him eating slowly and cleared her throat. "What's your name?"

"If I told you, I'd have to kill you." He gave her a long cold look. It was as if he'd turned to ice. "As an Army brat, you'd know all about classified information, so don't ask me again, and when we get stateside don't ask your dad. It's safer you don't know."

Annie glared at him. "Well, I can't yell out 'hey you' every time I need to get your attention. Make something up."

"Sure, I can do that." He changed as if slowly defrosting, shrugged, and stared into space for a beat. "You can call me Dave."

CHAPTER SEVEN

As they traveled the rest of the day and into the night, Annie took in the man beside her. He stood at least six-five with broad shoulders. His dark brown hair was cut short, and his eyes were so intense they took her breath away and reminded her of the darkest blue sky before nightfall. He'd broken his nose at one time, and she doubted the scars on his chin and above his eye were the only ones on his body. He was a warrior and, she had to admit, to-die-for handsome, and he'd use his body to protect her. Arrogant maybe, but she felt safe with him and had fallen asleep and woken when he'd pulled up behind a collection of houses. Heavily armed men had rushed out and gassed up the vehicle from cans. They'd all peered at her through the window but she'd remained covered up with only her eyes showing during the trip on the chance they ran into a roadblock. Dave removed his night-vision goggles, climbed out of the sedan, stretched, and then walked around and opened the door for her.

"Keep my body at your back at all times." He took her by the arm and the men surrounded them as they entered a small dwelling.

The house smelled of sweat, potatoes, and the same aromatic coffee. A woman came out of a back room but said nothing as she waved them to a table. As soon as Annie sat down, hot food arrived, with bread and the same yellow coffee. Dave spoke to a man in fast Arabic and gave him a wad of bills before sitting at the table with his back to the wall. Armed men guarded the door but Dave's attention shifted all around as he ate his meal.

They'd driven in virtual silence, although he'd been in communication with someone by the name of Terabyte. At times they'd veered off-road and bumped over uneven farmland or driven behind buildings and waited as a convoy drove past. It was as if he sensed when trouble was approaching. She'd been too intimidated by him to ask questions. What had he meant by "I'm the only weapon you'll need"? Annie kept her head down and ate slowly, eyeing him from under her lashes. He acted like a robot, as if he never tired. They'd been driving for hours, stopping only when nature called, and apart from thick black stubble, he looked as fresh as when they'd left the last town. His strength was formidable and when he'd lifted her over his shoulder, it had been like hitting a brick wall of solid muscle. His handsome face always had a stern expression, but then at times his eyes danced with amusement. He'd also treated her with respect and gentleness. There was obviously a nice guy under the shell of a hardened soldier. There had to be a reason. She wondered if he was a family man. She sipped the coffee. It gave her a rush of caffeine and, feeling much better, she met his scrutinizing gaze. "Are you married?"

"Negative." Dave refilled his cup and his gaze moved over her and then back to his plate. "Of all the questions you could have asked me, you want to know if I'm married." He continued to eat, shaking his head.

That went well. Annie shrugged. "Just making conversation. It's obvious the mission is classified, so asking you anything is a waste of time, but are the long silences really necessary?"

"It's okay to talk in the vehicle but remaining silent will save your life." Dave lifted his head but his attention was constantly moving from door to window. "Muslim women don't speak to men in this area, and as you're dressed as one, you should act the part, plus if anyone hears your accent, they'll kill you. We're in the heart of a rebel militia stronghold. The people helping us are placing themselves in danger by just speaking to us."

The reality of the situation hit Annie like a sledgehammer. She'd been under the impression that after so long, they'd moved out of danger. She clasped her hands together to stop them trembling. "I'm sorry I didn't understand how much danger we're in. I thought we were well away from the people who'd kidnapped me."

"Nope, the bounty on us will be high." Dave pushed his plate away and then pulled out his weapon, checked the load and his ammunition. "I'm in communication with someone who'll guide us out of trouble, but apart from a few friendlies who can be bought for a price by both sides, we're on our own."

"I see." Annie refilled her cup. "So, this could be our last meal for a time?"

"Yeah, but these people will give us some food and supplies." Dave checked his backpack. "I still have cheese. It keeps well but I'm restricted for space. I have a sniper rifle and will need to pack more ammo and the US bills into my backpack. There's not room for much else. My backpack is crucial to our survival, so you'll have to keep it safe." He gave her a wink. "Which means if we meet up with anyone suspicious on the road, you'll hide it under your robes. No man will touch you. They'll think your pregnant. We'll ask for another bag to carry the food. It's lucky it's winter. We'd never make it in summer." He stiffened as a man walked into the room.

The man spoke in rapid Arabic and handed him two bags. Annie waited for the man to leave and looked at Dave. "Food and ammo, right?"

"Yeah, and we need to go." Dave swapped cheese from his backpack and replaced it with ammunition. He inspected three grenades and placed them inside a pocket in the backpack and then took out a pair of night-vision goggles. "Take the food. We need to leave right now. Eyes down, don't look at anyone."

They hurried to the Audi and Annie stowed his backpack at her feet, the food and ammo went behind them under a blanket. She clipped in her seatbelt as Dave pulled on the night-vision goggles and took off at speed. "Is there a problem?"

"Maybe." He pressed his ear. "Terabyte, do you copy? What have we got?"

There was a pause as he listened to the transmission coming through his earpiece and then Dave turned suddenly off the road and headed across the barren landscape. The old car bumped and leapfrogged over the uneven ground. They moved at full speed and Dave spun the wheel, sliding the old sedan behind a small clump of trees. The movement had kicked up a cloud of dirt, which settled over the vehicle in an orange dust.

"Grab the food." Dave shrugged into his backpack, slung the other bag over one shoulder, and took her hand. He took off at full tilt toward a pile of rocks.

He moved so fast Annie had to suck in huge breaths to keep going. Her legs cramped but she kept running. As they got closer, she could see the ruins of a building made from mud bricks. Part of it still stood but most had been damaged. Bullet holes riddled one wall in a sickening show of violence. Heart pounding at a million beats a second, she allowed Dave to drag her up the side using the broken bricks as steps. She stood panting, bent over with her hands on her knees, sure her lungs would burst.

"Stay down, we have company." Dave scanned the building, checking the gaps, and then pushed her toward one. He pulled a box from his backpack, clicked it open, and in seconds had constructed a rifle and set it up, the muzzle fitting neatly between the bricks. He looked down at her and then handed her his sidearm. "If I go down, you might need this. Don't let them take you alive. These guys don't negotiate."

Dragging in deep breaths, she nodded and hunched down. Her mouth was so dry she couldn't form words. She pulled out a canteen of water, took a sip, and then handed it up to him. "What are you going to do?"

"Nothing." He shrugged. "They might drive past. The sedan looks like it's been there for a while with the dust all over it. It depends if the friendlies give us up or not. You never know. Out here nothing is certain. You can't trust anyone except me." He removed his goggles and stowed them in his backpack. "We wait and see." He pressed his com. "Terabyte, do you copy? We're in position. I'll wait here for the convoy to pass. Check in at twenty-four hundred."

When the sound of trucks rumbled through the night, Annie couldn't stop shaking. Fear grabbed her and her teeth chattered. She gripped the bag of food and hunkered down, but out in the middle of nowhere with only a few mud bricks for protection, terror had her by the throat. As the trucks moved closer and headlights moved across the landscape, a warm hand closed over her shoulder and squeezed. The hand stayed there, like a shield of protection.

"It's going to be okay. Take deep breaths, close your eyes. Stay calm." Dave's soothing voice had a strange calming effect on her. "They might shoot up the Audi but they don't know we're here."

Annie nodded. And then all hell broke loose. A spotlight swept the countryside back and forth and moved over the ruined house before settling on the car. The convoy stopped and gunfire rang out as automatic weapons sent thousands of rounds into the Audi. Unable to catch her breath, Annie closed her hand over Dave's and squeezed. She could feel the tension radiating from him, but he remained like a statue watching in silence. The noise went on forever and then loud raucous laughter came from the militia. After what seemed like a lifetime, the trucks rumbled off into the distance.

"Okay, we need to move." Dave stripped down his rifle and packed it away. "Ready?"

Petrified, Annie couldn't move. She just stared at him as he peeled her fingers from around the handle of the Glock. Her heart pounded in her ears and her legs refused to obey her. She opened her mouth but no words came out.

"You did good." Dave slid down to sit beside her. He took her hand and rubbed it between his own. "We all go into shock the first time we come under fire. You'll be fine." He stood, pulled on his backpack, and picked up all the bags. "Wait here, I'll see if the sedan is drivable."

Shaking like a bowl of Jell-O, Annie watched him move away and almost disappear in the dark, his long flowing robes covered special ops camouflage, which blended in with the sandy landscape. She wondered why he'd come to save her with only a robe covering his uniform. If the militia caught him, they'd torture him for days. She noticed a flashlight and made out Dave under the back of the car. The light flicked over the vehicle for a few seconds before he jumped inside and started it up. When he drove it toward her, she started down the building. Her feet went from under her and the air shot from her lungs as she landed flat on her back. Dazed and trying just to breathe, she stared at a million stars in a black endless sky.

"What part of 'stay here' didn't you understand?" Dave checked her over and stared into her eyes.

The look of concern for her calmed Annie's nerves. She couldn't resist touching his arm. "I'm sorry. Don't get so mad."

"I'll do my best." Dave's arms went around her as he lifted her and carried her to the car. "The Audi's toast. The fuel tank is leaking but I stuck a twig in it. We might make it to the next stop but it's going to be a rough ride. The tires are shredded." He sat her in the front seat, pulled out the canteen, and handed it to her. "Where's it hurting?" He pushed her hair back inside the burka and straightened it.

Heart missing a beat at his touch, Annie sipped the water and then handed it back to him. "Only my pride. I was trying to get down so we could get away from this place."

"Okay." He lifted her chin and stared into her eyes. "Remember what I told you. Obey my orders to the letter. Out here we're alone. If you'd broken a leg falling from the building, or your back, it would've been game over. We had a ten percent chance of making it out alive, and since they damaged the sedan, our odds have dropped. Do you want to see your family again, Annie?"

Embarrassed, Annie nodded. "Yes, of course I do."

"Then do as I tell you."

CHAPTER EIGHT

Texas

The front door to Shane Wolfe's house banged shut and his daughters Emily and Julie came hurtling down the passageway. He often wondered if his three, petite platinum-blonde daughters were related to elephants as they thundered through the house dropping bags and heading for the kitchen. He turned to the refrigerator and took out the milk. He looked at Anna, the baby of the family at two, sitting at the table with crayons spread all over, her little face screwed up with concentration. He sighed, wondering how he would cope raising three very strong-willed daughters alone. He pushed the thought aside and smiled as the girls tumbled into the kitchen, and headed to the sink to wash up. "How was school?"

"Well, I finish my work and sit staring at the wall most times." Emily took a jar of cookies from the bench and sat at the table. "It's boring. Can I be moved up a year? I know all this stuff."

Wolfe poured three glasses of milk and handed them around. "They put you up a year already. I can ask, but are you sure you want to be in with the older kids? They might bully you."

"Trust me, since the moment you walked into the science fair with me in uniform, no one would dare." Emily dug into the cookie jar. "My brain needs stimulation, Dad. I'll go crazy if I have to go through everything I already know for another entire year."

"Maybe if you didn't read all the books ahead of time, you might not get so bored." Julie shrugged. "I finish early too but just get out my homework and do it when everyone else is working on whatever. You should do the same."

"I do." Emily pulled a tragic face. "Can you do something? Please, Dad."

Wolfe blew out a sigh. "I'll see what I can do." He looked at Julie. "Watch Anna for a while for me. I have work to do." He turned to Emily. "Maybe go sit with your mom and tell her about your day. She's awake."

"She's not going to get better, is she?" Emily's eyes shone with tears. "What will we do without her?"

Wolfe pushed a hand through his hair. This was his Emily, brutally honest, straight down the line and there was no sugarcoating the truth with her. He'd explained Angela's illness in simple language a year earlier and just this morning had told his girls before they'd left for school that he'd be working from home from now on. Emily wasn't stupid and she already knew the answer. He could see her sadness growing every day. "No, she won't recover, and it's going to be difficult enough for her without us moping around. She knows the prognosis and she's worried we won't be able to cope. We need to let her know we'll all pitch in and get things done."

"I feel guilty I'm okay and she's so sick." Emily stared up at him and her lip quivered. "How long?"

The kids deserved honesty, preparing them for the inevitability would make it less of a shock. He shrugged. "Only God knows the answer, but not long."

"That's why you're here, isn't it? To be with her." Emily had gone sheet white. "She is so sick and I never know what to say to her. I'm frightened of saying the wrong thing."

Heart breaking, Wolfe sat down beside her and held her hand. "Tell her about your plans for the future. Ask her opinion. She'd like to be in your future, so paint a picture for her. Tell her all your plans and dreams, through school and beyond, like how you'd like to be a doctor."

"Okay, are you sure it won't make her sad?" Emily gripped his hand like a life preserver. "Should I tell her I'll take care of you?" She met his gaze. "I will. I'll help look after the girls. I'll cook and clean."

"I don't need looking after." Julie frowned at her. "I'll help as well. We all will, Dad. You know that, right?"

Wolfe cleared his throat. "What y'all need to do is finish school and go to college, but what you're doing now to help is all I need."

"What happens—after, when you have to go back to work. We'll be alone?" Emily dropped her hand. "Will you be okay, Dad?"

Wolfe stood, his hands trembled and he'd need to be the strong one. "We'll take it one day at a time. If needs be, I'll get a nanny for Anna. Maybe one who lives in and can be a housekeeper as well. It will make life easier. I can't expect your grandma to come by every day, even if she says she doesn't mind. She's not getting any younger." He pushed his hands in his pockets. "I have to get back to work. I'll be downstairs."

He turned away, switching from family man to Ninety-eight H's handler in a split second. While his children slept, he'd been working overnight organizing friendlies to assist in the extraction of Annie Parkes from a band of rogue militia. He hadn't been surprised at Ninety-eight H's ability to find cash and supplies, but the way he just up and walked into an enemy camp made him wonder if the man had the fear gene. Or maybe he had nothing to lose? He had no intel on his charge at all. He knew about his missions but his name, rank, and any other information were classified. After using the retinal scanner to enter his office, he sat down before the wall of screens and checked Ninety-eight H's progress. His instructions to keep moving toward the next contact point had been met with an affirmative. He'd sent them on a hazardous journey but he'd trust his own daughters with Ninety-eight H in the same circumstances. If anyone could get through enemy territory without being seen, it would be him. The red bleep on the screen was moving slowly. That couldn't be good. He rubbed his chin and checked the time. It was a little after four in Texas on Friday, which meant it was just after midnight in Syria on Sunday. Time for Ninety-eight H to check in. He pulled on his headset. "Ninety-eight H, do you copy?"

"Yeah. Man, I can tell time by you." Ninety-eight H sounded calm as usual but then he was always calm.

Wolfe checked the maps and messages. "You're a little off course. I'll give you a new set of coordinates."

"Negative. I know where I'm going." Ninety-eight H cleared his throat. *"Laying low to avoid hostiles. What's on the radar?"*

Wolfe checked the satellite feed. "The convoy on the highway west of your position is moving north. They won't be a problem. There's a single militia vehicle, military with a full load, heading in your direction. ETA twenty minutes. If you take cover behind the mound of rocks one hundred yards west, they'll roll right past you as they move through the valley."

"Copy. Yeah, well they'll be searching for us. They know we're in the Audi. We took fire when we left the last stopover. The old sedan limped here. It's toast. We're on foot and moving slow."

Wolfe dashed a hand through his hair. "Did the package come through in good condition?"

"Yeah, it's good. The wrapping is a bit messed up but it's okay." Ninety-eight H chuckled. *"Man, I could write a book about this mission. I've gotta go. I need to locate a more suitable vehicle. I'll check in at zero two hundred. Out."*

CHAPTER NINE

Syria

Dave squeezed Annie's hand as they plodded on through the night. Her need for encouragement was his excuse, but he'd felt a connection with her the moment their eyes had met. He swallowed hard. Relationships in his line of work were off limits, so he'd enjoy her company and keep the memory for the bad times ahead. Traveling over rough ground by moonlight wasn't easy for her and he wished he had another set of night-vision goggles to give her. The woman had grit. He'd give her that. Yeah, she'd been terrified under fire but that was a normal reaction. She'd recovered faster than expected, but after the sedan died, she'd kept pace with him and she hadn't complained, not once. He'd noticed her trying to disguise a limp and no doubt she'd be covered in bruises come morning, but maybe keeping her moving had been a blessing in disguise. His night-vision goggles picked out the rocky mound high on one side of a valley. From Terabyte's report, the way ahead was clear but a military truck was heading in their direction. He needed to get into position and pulled Annie along a little faster. "There's a truck coming this way. We need to make it up the side of the hill behind those rocks." He stopped walking and turned to her. "I'll leave something here to slow the truck down. There are grenades in the right-side pocket of my backpack. Pull one out for me."

"Me?" Annie looked at him wide-eyed. "What if I do something stupid and it explodes?"

Biting back a grin, Dave squeezed her hand before releasing it. "You have to pull the pin before it explodes and then we have two seconds to throw it. Just don't pull the pin."

Her hand trembled so much he could feel it as she tugged at the Velcro to lift the flap on the pocket, and lifted out a grenade between finger and thumb. He took it from her and sat it beside a small bush alongside the road. He'd use the bush as a marker, the landscape looked like the moon through his night-vision goggles, and the vegetation was sparce and dry. He took her hand again, her fingers cold against his palm. After the long walk she should be sweating. He glanced at her. "You're freezing. What are you wearing under the *abayah*?" He took in her blank expression. "The dress."

"Are you joking?" She pulled her hand away and glared at him. "I mean… really? We're stuck in the middle of nowhere with people trying to kill us and you're hitting on me?"

Dave snorted with laughter, unable to stop the wide grin spreading over his face. "Hitting on you? Nope, I wouldn't dare even if I wanted to." He held up both hands in mock surrender and then glanced back along the road, watching for any approaching headlights in the distance. "We're going to engage the enemy in about ten minutes and, trust me, the last thing on my mind right now is jumping your bones." He heaved in a breath and headed toward the hillside shaking his head in disbelief. "I'm concerned for your welfare; you shouldn't be so cold. Most women in these parts wear thick undergarments, from neck to knee in winter. I'm assuming you're not, as you're so frigid."

"Frigid?" Annie pulled on his arm. "Oh boy, you're good at double meanings. I'm not at all frigid. I might be freezing my butt off, but if you took the time to get to know me, you'd find that I'm a loyal and loving person." She stood staring at him, hands on hips. "They gave me undergarments but I figured if I was going to die, I'd die like an American, wearing a bra and panties. I did pull on the long black socks though, so I looked respectable in their eyes."

Admiring her fierce patriotism, Dave held out his hand. "I meant cold, Annie. I wasn't being sexist. I haven't got a sexist bone in my body."

"You're so hard to read." Annie stared into his eyes. "You have this look about you like a predator."

Dave shook his head. "Your instinct is right about me. I'm a highly skilled assassin, Annie. That's why your dad sent me to save you. Those guys out there are trying to kill us. Right now, it's kill or be killed. We could die in the next hour, so let's call a truce and be friends. For as sure as hell, I don't want to spend my last hours on earth arguing."

"I'd like that." She took his hand. "You certainly have a way with words, Dave."

Her hand was cold against his flesh as he started walking. "There's a town fifty clicks away. If we survive the next hour or so, I'll buy you some extra clothes. In the meantime, there's a blanket in the bag with the food. When we stop, wrap it around you and try to keep warm while I'm busy."

"Okay." Annie squeezed his hand and shuddered. "Jeez, it's hard talking to a man with green glowing eyes. I feel like I'm walking on the moon with an alien." She lifted her chin. "I'm sorry. I know you'd probably prefer to be home rather than risking your life for me."

"I'm following orders." Dave quickened the pace. "Stay close. The ground gets steep just ahead. We'll have to climb up to the top of the hill. There's cover up there."

"We can't possibly walk all the way to the border. I gather that's where we're heading, to Turkey? It's a little safer there, right?" Annie looked up at him, a determined look on her face.

Dave glanced down at her. "That's the plan. I'm hoping they'll send a bird to evac us from there if it's safe to land." He glanced behind him, checking for headlights in the distance. "I'm planning on commandeering the militia truck. It would be perfect. No one will stop us until they discover their men are missing. We'll have a few hours' start at least."

"Oh, yeah?" Annie snorted. "Like they'll just give it up to you without a fight."

Dave shrugged and pulled her up the hillside. "Oh, I expect a fight, but they won't be needing it when they're dead."

"Dead, huh?" Annie puffed along behind him. "Are you out of your mind? You won't be able to take on a truckload of militia alone."

Biting back a grin, he stopped and turned to her. "I've taken on more than a truckload of militia in my time. That's what I'm trained to do, Annie. One or twenty enemy soldiers, it makes no difference. I'll take them down. I never miss."

"Big words." Annie jogged along beside him. "You'd have to be the most arrogant man I've ever met. It's like talking to a machine. You don't care who lives or dies, do you?"

Taken aback, Dave pulled her the last few yards to a rocky outcrop and turned to face her. "Do I care about taking out men who will rape, torture, and murder you? No! Do I care about killing the men who dragged my spotter through the streets behind their vehicle and then beheaded him and stuck his head on a spike? No! In fact, I'm damn sure I'd kill them all twice if I was able." He pulled off his goggles and leaned down close to her face. "Do you have any idea what would have happened to you if I hadn't saved your sorry ass? You couldn't even come close to imagining the pain and suffering these people can inflict. It might have gone on for years before they tired of you." He sucked in a breath to calm his rising temper. "You know, it would be easier for me to put a bullet in your head now and just walk away. I could go dark and no one will find me, but with you along, that's impossible. Everyone will be looking for a young blonde American. You'll have a bounty on your head."

"So much for your orders." Annie crossed her arms and eyeballed him.

Dave shrugged. "They were my orders, Annie. Trust me, you're better off dead than falling into their hands."

She said nothing and just leaned against a boulder, staring at the ground.

Using his flashlight, Dave searched the area before finding a suitable place to hole up. He walked a few paces to another pile of rocks and then back. "Grab the blanket and sit here. Drink some water and we'll eat something while we wait." He pointed to a secluded spot. "If you need to pee. Go now, over there. You'll be able to use the flashlight. No one is on the road just now."

"What were you looking for in the rocks?" Annie took the flashlight from him.

Dave removed his backpack and set up his rifle. "Critters. They like to hide under things and in the cracks in rocks." He waved her away. "Hurry, we haven't much time. Once we see headlights coming down the road, it's game on."

He checked the range on his rifle, turning the gauges and lining up the road. He'd positioned them as far as possible from the range of an automatic rifle fired from the road. As Annie came back and sat where he'd suggested, he dropped down beside her and pulled out the blanket, food, and water. He smiled at her blank expression. It was as if the reality of their situation had finally sunk in. "Sorry for the reality check, but we're in serious trouble. When this goes down, we'll be moving fast. It's best you eat now even if you're not hungry. First rule is, eat when you can, sleep when it's safe, and keep one eye open." He cleared his throat and thought of something to say to her to ease the tension. "What I wouldn't do for a freshly brewed coffee with cream and sugar right now and an entire freshly baked peach pie."

"You're so good at smoothing things over. I'm not so good. My dad says I'm as stubborn as a mule and twice as ornery." She smiled at him. "I can change the subject too. Right now, a double-shot latte would go down just fine." She wrinkled her nose. "What they have here is very different to what I'm used to, but it's nice." Annie dived into the bag of dates and took the chunk of goat cheese he offered her.

"It's called *qahwa*, the wine of the desert, I believe." He ate slowly, one eye constantly on the road below them in the valley. "It gives the caffeine buzz and to be served it is a privilege, especially from the farmers we've been meeting. They have very little and shared their food with us."

"They were well compensated by the amount of money you gave them." Annie leaned out from her hiding place and peered at the road. "I thought I could hear something and now I see lights."

Dave pushed her gently back into the cover of the rocks and pulled the blanket tight around her legs. He handed her his sidearm. "Same as before, okay? If I go down, don't hesitate. Under the chin is best. You won't feel a thing." He squeezed her arm. "Don't look around the rock at what's happening, or they'll see you. Any movement will give away our position. Don't talk to me. When it's over I'll come get you. Understand?"

"Yes." She looked up at him anxiously, her face very pale under the moonlight. "Will you be close by?"

He pointed higher up. "I've set up my rifle up there. I'll have an advantage."

A calmness dropped over him as he climbed up the rocks and stretched out. He checked his scope and watched the truck rumble along the dusty road toward them. His heart slowed and all his focus was centered on his target. *Game on.*

CHAPTER TEN

Fear crept over Annie as the sound of the militia truck came closer. She pressed her back into the narrow fissure between the rocks and pulled the blanket up to her chin as if it would protect her. Dave's sidearm sat beside her within easy reach, the cold metal disappearing in the shadows. She touched it again to make sure it was there. Above her, Dave was like a statue. He didn't make a sound or move an inch. The rumbling engine came closer and then she heard a low *phutt* from above followed by three more. Dave was firing at the truck and his rifle hardly made a sound. Another *phutt*, and an explosion shook the earth. The sky lit up and debris showered down on her pinging across the rocks. She covered her head with her arms and hoped it was over but Dave was firing again.

Trembling all over, she waited, but the long silence that followed frightened her. Had he been hit? Was the militia heading her way? She eased her hand over the dirt and her fingers touched the weapon. Heart pounding, she closed her palm around the cold handle. She clamped her mouth shut but couldn't stop her teeth chattering. When gravel rolled down the rocks and Dave came into view, he looked different. The robotic man was back with a vengeance. He said nothing, just packed up his rifle and dropped the backpack at her feet. She looked up at him. "Did you get them?"

"Yeah." Dave held out a hand for the sidearm. "Wait here. I'll roll the bodies into the dry riverbed beside the road. They'll be out of sight for the next patrol. When I'm done, I'll drive the truck as close to you as possible and come get you. Stay here. You don't need to see this, okay?"

Annie stared at his grim expression. "I'll come and help you. I'm not squeamish."

"No!" Dave turned away, pulling on his night-vision goggles. "Stay here. That's an order. Keep watch—militia use this road—and call out if you see any lights. I'm going to be busy for a while." He hurried away through the rocks and down the side of the valley without making a sound.

Annie watched him go, his long robes flowing. He'd soon become a ghostly shadow moving fast toward the truck in the middle of the road. Alongside a crater, small fires had broken out in the tufts of dry grass and a small bush was alight, sending flames leaping into the night. The flames danced in the wind, sending an eerie glow across the fallen militia. Smoke from the burning grass filled the air with the smell of bonfires as it drifted across the road obscuring her view. From time to time, she could see Dave moving around, dragging bodies across the road and rolling them out of sight. She swallowed the bile threatening to fill her mouth. It had all become so horribly real. Dave had killed to protect her. She hunkered down but kept a watch on the road in both directions. After half an hour, maybe more, she noticed lights on the horizon. Panic gripped her. Someone was coming fast. The lights bobbing up and down on the uneven, potholed track were minutes away. Had Dave seen them? Throwing caution to the wind, she cupped her mouth. *Will he be able to hear me?* "Incoming."

She repeated the call as loud as she could and watched frozen in terror as the militia truck, flag flying high, came into view. As she looked back at the road, Dave had vanished, but the oncoming truck had slowed and she could make out a gun atop the vehicle with one soldier behind it. The truck came to a standstill, the headlights picking out the crater in the road and the debris scattered all around. Annie held her breath as the door opened with a rusty squeak. From the interior light, she made out two men. One climbed out and walked toward the other truck, his rifle held shoulder high. He moved around the truck with caution, peering in the cab and the back, all the time yelling at the others.

The man's attention went to the riverbed. He stood on the edge and then lowered his weapon. He started screaming and waving his arms around at his companions. His flashlight lit up the roadway and he yelled again. The next moment, the other men ran toward him and they all headed down to the riverbed. Where was Dave? Had they seen him? She gripped the rock until her nails broke and stared into the darkness. Her stomach tightened in fear and nausea made her gag but she couldn't stop looking as the flashlight moved from side to side, stopping occasionally and then moving again.

Annie waited, heart in her mouth, straining her eyes for any movement. The next second, three shots rang out, echoing through the valley like a death knell. She let out an uncontrollable sob. Dear Lord, help her. They'd found him.

CHAPTER ELEVEN

Texas

Wolfe checked the clock again for the tenth time in a minute. Ninety-eight H should have checked in ten minutes ago. He scanned the screens. His operative's red blip pulsed in a stationary position, and from the satellite feed, he could clearly see two militia trucks and spot fires spreading along the road. He rubbed the back of his neck. If the militia truck was the transport Ninety-eight H had planned to obtain, he'd picked a good spot for an ambush. In a valley, the road passed through a rugged barren hillside. If he'd taken out the men on the trucks, he might be waiting to make sure it was all clear before proceeding. He stood and paced up and down the length of his new office, fully equipped with the best communications the military could offer. He had no option but to wait. Contacting his operative could cause a fatal distraction. It was twelve after six in Texas and he'd eaten dinner with his kids and spent some time with his wife.

He never liked leaving her alone for a second but since connecting her to the morphine drip she was rarely awake. It tore him apart watching her waste away but there was nothing he could do to save her and God knows they'd tried everything. Finally, she'd insisted he take her home and refused to undergo anymore experimental treatments. He'd wanted to fight until the end but had respected her wishes. He could see the life draining from her, and as much as it would break his heart for her to leave him, as a doctor he knew it would be a blessing. She'd suffered long enough.

He'd been staring at the satellite picture but not seeing it and blinked as the trucks moved off together and the red dot moved along the road. Did the militia have Ninety-eight H's body? There would be no way they'd take him alive. The voice in his earpiece startled him as Ninety-eight H checked in. He heaved a sigh of relief. "Copy. I was ready to write your obituary. You're giving me an ulcer."

"I'd just taken out a band of militia and then we had company. Long story, but now we have two trucks. If Uncle Sam does a flyby, make sure they have my coordinates, I don't want to be taken out by friendly fire. I'm flying a militia flag here."

Wolfe stared at the screen array. "This is a covert operation, and if it wasn't, I couldn't risk breaking radio silence to contact anyone outside this office. You and I have a direct secured line but anything can be hacked."

"Sure. We'll keep heading west. Once we reach the outskirts of the next town, I'll ditch the flags and we'll use one truck. We'll need a safe house. I haven't had any shut-eye for forty-eight hours and the package needs warm clothes." He paused for a beat. *"Ammo, food, and clean water. A couple of extra cans of gas as well, if possible."*

Wolfe had anticipated the request and made contact to friendlies in the next town. He'd arranged for three different locations for them to stay. They'd have to move around to avoid capture. He explained the deal to the unimpressed Ninety-eight H.

"Three moves? I was expecting to hole up for a couple of days and wait for the search to die down and then head west."

"You'll never get past the movement of the hostiles. From the speed they're moving, you'll need to hide for three days at least in the town before attempting to leave."

"Copy that."

Hesitant to ask, Wolfe cleared his throat. "Ah… how's the package handling the Pony Express? It's pretty rough going out there for someone raised in a city."

"Better than expected." Ninety-eight H chuckled. *"She's a feisty one, and we fight like cats and dogs. She's not at all what I'd expected. She's dead on her feet but hasn't complained once. We're getting along okay now. Seems we've gotten over yelling at each other, or maybe it's because she's just too darn exhausted to fight, I don't know, but I'm actually starting to admire her."*

Wolfe grinned. He'd heard about the general's daughter. Strong willed, feisty, and set in her ways. Had she melted the iceman in a few days? "That doesn't surprise me. She's a beautiful young woman."

"Hey, I said 'admire' not 'in love.' I've pushed her like a drill sergeant and she's done everything right. She deserves my admiration, but trust me, love isn't in the picture. A man in my profession doesn't get to love anyone." Ninety-eight H sighed. *"She calls me Dave, by the way. A nice, safe generic name, don't you think?*

"Well, Ninety-eight H is a bit of a mouthful." Surprised by his good humor, Wolfe smiled to himself. "Does she have a pseudonym? If so, what do you call her?"

"No need. The militia know who she is. I call her Annie." He could hear the smile in Dave's voice. "*At the moment, her eyes are as wide as saucers. She's never driven a truck before but is doing okay. There's not much she can run into out here."*

Wolfe scrutinized the satellite picture, moving in on anything suspicious. "I'm the only one watching the screen, but if I need a break, I'll still be wearing my earpiece. Contact me if you need clarification of enemy movements, but as far as I can see, you're clear to the next town. From the intelligence, the militia is moving all its troops south. You should be good to go unless you meet up with a few stragglers but there's nothing on the radar."

"Copy, I'll check in on the hour until we make the town and meet up with the friendlies. I'll get details later. If it's safe, I'm getting some shut-eye and you should too."

"Copy." Wolfe pressed his com and disconnected. "Stay safe out there, Dave."

CHAPTER TWELVE

Syria

As the first rays of sunlight came over the top of the hillside, Annie blinked at the dust cloud kicked up by Dave's truck. *Sore* didn't describe her eyes. They'd gone way past sore and into the dragged-out-and-rolled-in-sand feeling. Peering through the eye slit in the burka didn't help, it covered her sight each time the truck hit a bump in the road. So tired. Exhaustion pulled at her and the thought of a warm bed had taken up residence in her mind. She'd discovered pain had a significant value in sleep deprivation by keeping her wide awake. The agony burning in her back from falling down the hillside had increased tenfold, but determined not to look weak by complaining, she kept her foot down on the gas and gripped the wheel.

The heavy truck was like wrestling an alligator and when the wheels hit ruts in the road, they suddenly had minds of their own. She'd never have made it through traffic, and time and again the truck bounced off the dirt track and into the scrub before she regained control. How much longer did Dave intend to keep going without a break? It was as if he'd completely forgotten about her following behind him. Then there was the smell. The truck stank of unwashed bodies and bad breath. The thick musky odor seemed to hang in the air like a disgusting fog. She'd probably carry the stink on her for days. Opening the window wasn't an option. It was freezing outside and the windows offered her a modicum of cover if anyone happened to drive by. Dave had taken a hat from one of the dead mercenaries and insisted she wear the stinking thing, as it seemed the militants didn't allow women to drive, along with an entire list of things he insisted she not do when they met anyone along the way.

A curl of panic grabbed her as Dave's truck slowed and he pulled into a clump of trees. She hadn't seen much vegetation for miles and stared all around expecting someone to jump out at them. She drove off the road and pulled up behind him waiting for instructions. He'd made it very clear she wasn't to leave the truck unless he was close by. She'd come to the realization he'd take a bullet for her. How did men do that for people they hardly knew? She'd been surrounded by the military all her life but hadn't fully realized the dedication to duty existed at such a high level. The Secret Service maybe, but from what she surmised, Dave was a sniper. Not that he said anything but after he'd taken down nine men with an equal number of shots and hit a grenade from a long distance, she believed him when he said he never missed. He was fearless and walked into danger as if nothing could harm him. With all hell breaking out around them, he made her feel safe.

When Dave waved her down from the truck, she tossed the hat inside the cab, grabbed her canteen of water, and ran toward him. It was so cold. The icy chill seeped through her thin clothes and her teeth chattered. "What's up?"

"We have time to stretch our legs and then you'll be riding with me." Dave walked toward the trees and then turned to her. "I'll rig up my backpack so you can wear it under your dress. I have to hide the weapons. Carrying US military issue and wearing a uniform will have us both killed. I'll stay covered up, and once we get into the next town, we'll ditch the truck and I'll find something else."

Annie looked at his grim expression. "Is it safe there?"

"Safer than out here alone." Dave rubbed his chin and looked at her. "I have contacts in the next town. We'll be able to get some rest and hopefully find you some warm clothes to wear under the dress. We're still Americans and worth money to anyone handing us over to the militants. I might get away with the disguise and I speak the language, but you don't and your skin hasn't seen a lick of sun. You'll need to keep your head down. I mean right down. Your blue eyes will stick out so keep your attention fixed on the ground. Follow my feet, don't speak, or look at anyone we meet. That's normal around these parts, especially when I'll tell them you're my wife and heavily pregnant. They should ignore you completely. The weight of my backpack will add to the deception." He waved to a dense bush. "That's the best I can do for a bathroom. I'll break out some supplies and then we'll have to go. I'll need to check in again soon. I'll have more info then."

The numbness that had surrounded her when she'd realized that Dave had killed nine men without hesitation to protect her just got another coating. She headed for the bushes. She'd be in mortal danger in a crowd of hostiles and it terrified her. Her mind was already having problems making sense of the carnage she'd witnessed. She'd been sure the militants had killed Dave, and seeing his flowing robes appear as he walked around the truck had brought tears of relief to her eyes. He'd moved the bodies, jumped into the truck and driven to collect her as if nothing had happened. He hadn't said a word about the incident until she'd asked him. He'd been so matter of fact, as if he'd just taken out the garbage. In truth, Dave had been incredibly brave or completely crazy. He'd laid down in the ditch with the dead bodies and when the three men from the other truck had checked on their comrades, he'd just rolled over and killed them. Just like that. She swallowed hard. Heck, he must have nerves of steel.

She returned to where he was sitting on a rock, fiddling with his backpack. She sat down beside him. "Thanks for looking after me. I know this isn't what you do. I've heard my dad talking about snipers being dropped behind enemy lines and having to find their way back to an evac point. Nothing specific, just how much he admires them. I'm guessing that's what you do. Look, I know you can't tell me anything about yourself, and that's okay, but when this is all over and you return to the States, come by and we'll go for a real coffee. I'm sure you know where I live." She pulled off her burka and smiled at him. "My treat."

"I'll hold you to that, ma'am. Once this mission is over, I'm planning on staying stateside for a time. I'd really like to see you again." Dave searched her face. "You know that few women would want to spend time with someone like me. I'm a mass murderer with no conscience. If I wasn't in the military. I'd be on death row somewhere by now."

What's with the ma'am? Annie took in the man beside her. *Handsome* was an adjective that didn't come close. She shook her head. "I don't see you that way. You don't kill unless you have to and out here it's kill or be killed. I can see that. I'm not stupid. I see a brave, loyal, and fearless man."

"Uh-huh. All that and we've only known each other for a few days." He gave her a slow smile that lit up his eyes. "You're a pain in the ass but you're growing on me." He tucked a strand of hair behind her ear. "Let's hope we survive the next few days. Once we make it to the border we'll be evacuated. And then I'll hold you to that coffee."

CHAPTER THIRTEEN

With his sidearm hidden by his flowing robes and head covered, Dave headed into the town. Its size was substantial, which was good and made it easier to hide. He had his orders and a rough idea of where to go. They'd head for an area hit by a series of car bombs and dump the truck. The place would be deserted and Terabyte had organized a meet with a friendly. Not that he trusted anyone, but with Annie along he had no choice. She needed sleep and a decent meal. They had a long way to go before they'd be safe. He pulled the truck into the curb. They'd walk from here. He could see the bombed-out shells of the storefronts Terabyte had described about fifty yards away.

He glanced at her. He liked Annie and that was a problem because he'd made up his mind long ago not to form any permanent relationships. He'd had girlfriends from all over the world, but the moment he'd explained his career came first, they never returned his calls. He shrugged. Maybe Annie would be different?

"Is there a problem?" Annie was staring at him through the slit in her burka. "You've gone all serious and now you're shaking your head."

Dave glanced at her. "Please don't ask me what I'm thinking. I hate it when people ask that."

Annie's eyes flashed in annoyance. "Sorry, I thought you'd seen something; you know, like a band of militia with their rifles trained on us."

"I'd tell you if I did." Dave slid on his sunglasses and adjusted his headgear. "This looks like the right place. Wait here, I'll grab the bags and come round and lift you down."

"I'll be fine." Annie's hand went to the door.

Dave rolled his eyes. "No, you won't, and if you fall over, you might damage my rifle. That could mean life or death to us right now. Wait here."

He heard her exasperated sigh as he climbed out, grabbed the bags, and headed around the hood. After dropping the bags on the ground, he opened the door, lifted her down, and set her on her feet. She swayed slightly under the weight of his backpack but straightened, holding her back. He smiled, she sure looked pregnant. He gathered the bags and they moved not so swiftly to the gutted store on one corner. "We'll wait here. They'll be along soon, I hope."

He scanned the area, keeping his body between her and the street. He heard the vehicle before it came into view. An old battered sedan covered in dust pulled up beside them. A man leaned out the window and spoke to him in Arabic.

"Hurry, get in before anyone sees you." He gestured with his arms. "We have a safe place but it's ten minutes from here."

Dave helped Annie into the car, dropped in his bags beside her and climbed into the front passenger seat. He nodded at the man. "What do I call you?"

Terabyte had given him a name. If the man didn't respond with the correct reply, he'd end up collateral damage just like the others. He waited, his hand slipping beneath his robes to his sidearm.

"They call me Farid." The man smiled at him. "Don't worry, there are many here who do not agree with the militants." He waved a hand to encompass the ruins. "This was a thriving town and now we live in fear. How long will it last? I'm not sure anyone will survive."

Dave nodded and relaxed a little. "Did you find the supplies I asked for, particularly clothes for my wife?"

"We have most of what you need and will find more before you leave. We didn't have much time. I'm sure you understand things aren't easy to come by at the moment."

"I understand." Dave cleared his throat. "We need a safe place to rest. My wife is exhausted."

"It's not far now." Farid smiled at him. "I think this place will please you."

Farid drove at a fast pace along damaged roads, until they came to side streets with people milling around. It was as if civilization had just been switched back on. As they drove, slower now, Dave scanned the streets, familiarizing himself with the area. If they wanted to leave in a hurry, he'd need to have some idea of which way to go. Surprised to see so many people out on a Sunday, he turned to Farid. "Is it usual to have so many people out and about on a Sunday?"

"They get out when they can and stores open when the militia has left the town. The militants have no thought for anyone's property. All believe they are entitled to take what they want without payment." Farid shook his head. "We have rocks and they have guns, so we survive any way we can."

Dave frowned. "Perhaps, I can help. Do you have a resistance?"

"We do indeed." Farid's expression became animated. He pulled to the curb and turned to him. "There will be a small patrol left to guard the militia's supplies, usually ten men. Some stay in the storeroom and others drive around killing people who get in their way."

Watching all around, Dave thought for a beat. It would be to his advantage to gain these people's trust. He sighed. "If I cleared the area, how would you get rid of the bodies and the trucks?"

"Leave that to us." Farid smiled broadly, his eyes dancing with excitement. "We're expert at hiding things. It would take no time at all to dig a pit. We have an excavator at the landfill. Removing garbage has been a problem here and digging a pit would be a normal thing to do. We'll bury the men and the trucks if necessary and then cover them with garbage. There is no shortage of that here."

"You should take their weapons as well and protect yourselves." Dave moved his attention back to Farid. "And ammo?" He gave the details of a variety of bullets he'd require in the hope they could source some for his rifle.

"I will find what you need. They are on the list of requirements we received." Farid clasped his hands together. "I already have people searching for items on your list." He looked all around. "It's safe to drive on, no one is around." He pulled back onto the dusty road.

The deal would be off without ammo. Dave had no intention of disposing targets with his bare hands, although he could without a problem, but the chances of being discovered would be greater, and he had Annie to think about now. "Okay, we'll help each other but I must leave here as soon as the militia have cleared out. My wife has little time left and we must get home."

"We have a deal, my friend." Farid stopped outside a store that displayed rolls of material and dressmaker's dummies draped in various garments. "This is the place. It is over the store and very safe. Bars on the doors and windows. No one can get inside."

Dave frowned. "How do we get out?"

"By the roof." Farid grinned. "The buildings are close together. You can easily step from one to another across the rooftops but no one will expect to find you here. Come inside. People seeing you coming and going will think you are here to buy clothes. Just the right place for your wife to visit. Everything she needs is here. You as well. Go inside. They are expecting you. I must go but I'll be back very soon."

Dave collected the bags and led Annie into the store. It was like going back in time. He waited for a man to come out from the back, with one hand on his sidearm and Annie safely behind him. He peered at the small man. "We are friends of Farid."

"Yes, come this way. The rooms upstairs belonged to my son and his wife but they were killed last year in an explosion. We live on the other side. It's small but has everything you need." He glanced at Annie and then back at Dave. "There is food and hot water. Clothes for your wife as ordered." The man paused for a few seconds as if waiting for something. "I'm sure you'll be comfortable."

Dave had wads of cash in his pockets, just in case he'd have to leave his bag behind. All the US bills he'd stashed in his backpack. They'd need cash to get out of trouble if the evac went to hell. He slid his hand inside his pocket and pulled out folded bills. He handed them to the man and his eyes widened. Dave smiled at him. "More than enough for your trouble don't you agree?"

"You are very generous." The man held the wad of bills as if it were precious jewels.

Dave hadn't been born yesterday. He understood loyalty was a commodity easily bought and betrayal rampant in this neck of the woods. He removed his sunglasses and eyeballed him. "I'm no fool. I can make you rich or dead. It's your decision. Are we clear?"

"Most certainly." The man tucked the money away and waved a hand toward the back of the shop. "Through the curtain and up the stairs, the door on the left. You are most welcome in my humble home."

Moving to the steps, Dave motioned Annie to wait. He leaned into her and dropped his voice to just above a whisper. "Watch him. If he goes for his phone, tell me. If he does anything suspicious, tell me. I'll clear the room. Don't move until I come get you." When she nodded, he turned away and checked every step, looking for tripwires and found none. He moved into the room and searched the small space with a bathroom, noting the pull-down steps leading to the roof. Heat from a fireplace brushed his face and a savory smelling concoction came from a pot bubbling over the flames. A double bed and a small table and two wooden chairs took up the rest of the space. He went back to the stairs and waved Annie toward him.

The shop owner had supplied many of the things he'd requested. A set of warm clothes sat folded on one end of the bed. He looked through them, finding three changes of women's undergarments and a clean dress and burka. He didn't need anything. He carried extra clothes in his backpack. Food included dates, cheese, and bread. He checked through a box of supplies and found a jar of instant coffee. *Ambrosia.* When Annie came into the room puffing like a train, he locked the door and helped her out of her dress in order to remove the backpack. His gaze moved over the purple bruises coming out over her lower back and elbows. She'd been hurt in the fall and hadn't said a word. He ground his teeth. "Why didn't you tell me you were injured?"

"I didn't want to slow us down." Annie picked up the clothes and examined them. She seemed oblivious to the fact she was in her underwear.

Dave averted his eyes and waved to his backpack. "I have a med kit. Morphine and other meds."

"I don't need morphine just yet. Tylenol maybe?"

Dave kept his eyes on the floor. "Sure. I'll find you some and then check on the food." He waved her toward the bathroom. "I'm guessing you'll want to wash up first? Maybe take the clean clothes in with you?"

"You can look at me, Dave. I wear less than this on the beach." Annie held the clothes to her chest. "Do you have a comb?"

"Sure." Dave pulled off his robe and took a comb from a pocket and handed it to her. "Don't use all the hot water. It's a luxury here." He cleared his throat. "If you need to rinse out your underwear, I'll rig up a line in front of the fire. I'll be doing mine."

"Copy that." Annie grinned at him and hurried into the bathroom.

CHAPTER FOURTEEN

The tiny bathroom had no shower but a tin hip bath with a plug in the bottom sat under the taps beside a toilet. The rust-stained hand basin had a small cabinet above, containing a few toiletries. They'd supplied the essentials, soap, shampoo, and towels. Annie examined the sponge on the sink. It appeared clean enough and after soaping it up in the hand basin and washing it thoroughly, she added a small amount of hot water to the hip bath and bathed. She couldn't imagine how Dave could possibly use the hip bath as she'd had enough trouble getting cleaned up, and washing her hair under the tap had been a nightmare. She'd dried off as best she could and then rinsed her underwear in the sink. After dressing in the thick undergarments they'd kindly supplied, which covered her from neck to ankles, she combed her hair and, teeth chattering, returned to the other room.

She hung her underwear on the makeshift washing line above the mantel and took the blanket Dave offered her and draped it around herself. She smiled at him. "Thanks." She peered into the pot he'd been stirring on the fire. "What do you think that is?"

"I've no idea." He covered the pot and looked up at her. "Best we don't ask and just eat it. It's been simmering for some time and smells okay. I'd say this is breakfast, lunch, and dinner. The dates and cheese are staples around this area. Fresh bread is a bonus." He gave her a long look. "When I'm in the bathroom, don't go near the window or open the door if anyone knocks. They wouldn't expect you to speak to anyone, so just tell me if anyone shows." He stood and removed his flowing robes. "Do you mind, if I strip down? I won't be able to turn around in the bathroom."

Shaking her head, Annie averted her gaze. "Go right ahead. You can't do anything to embarrass me."

He said nothing but gave a little snort.

Annie dragged one of the chairs over to the fire and sat down. As she combed her wet hair over the heat, she snuck a peek at him. He looked so different in his fatigues, and when he undressed and stood there in brown skivvies, she had to force her attention back to the fire. She'd been surrounded by Marines all her life and the size of him didn't intimidate her at all, but his raw masculinity made her toes curl in a good way. She relaxed when he closed the bathroom door and got up to search around for plates. Hunger gnawed at her belly and whatever it was in the pot cooking, she didn't care anymore.

It took Dave less than ten minutes to wash up and return in fresh skivvies, his hair wet and glossy like a seal. He'd washed his clothes as well and hung them to dry. When he'd dressed, she handed him a plate and he scooped out food for both of them. Annie tasted the meal with apprehension, but the savory meat dish was okay, very oily and the meat tough but it filled her belly along with some of the bread. Dave had offered her half the loaf but she'd pulled a little off and handed it back to him. She'd heard his stomach growling since they'd met but he'd always offered her the food and eaten just enough to survive. "You need to eat. I've never eaten much and we need you to be strong. I'll tell you if I'm hungry, so please eat your fill."

"I've money to buy more food now we're in the city." Dave dipped the bread into the gravy. "We'll be sick of cheese and dates by the time we leave but they're plentiful here. They're good enough to survive on for some time. I'll make sure to take some with us when we leave here."

Annie took the kettle from the fire and filled two cups, adding the instant coffee. She handed him one. "No sugar or cream but it's better than nothing."

"Ambrosia." Dave sniffed the brew. "You'd better go get some sleep when you're done. I'll fix the dishes and take the first watch."

As Annie had slept in the truck, she shook her head. "Nope, I'm wide awake. I insist you get a few hours shut-eye. How long has it been since you've slept?"

"I've lost track but I'll only need four hours." He inserted an earpiece in one ear. "I'll check in first." He handed her his Glock. "If anyone forces their way through that door when I'm asleep, don't hesitate. I'll wake but you'll have the edge. Understand?"

Annie took the weapon and nodded. "I know what to do."

"Good." He stood and walked into the bathroom.

Annie could hear his voice speaking low, even his communications were top secret. When he returned, he made no comment about his conversation and just laid his sidearm on the pillow, climbed into bed, and in seconds was asleep. She stared at him. His breathing came slow and steady. For the first time since he'd rescued her, he looked at peace. She watched him for ages, it was hard to believe that handsome face hid a warrior inside. Checking her feelings, she turned her head away, stood, and went to the sink to clean the dishes. She'd heard how women fell head over heels for their rescuers and it wasn't hard to understand why. She figured it was the attention. She'd had few boyfriends, mostly at college and the casual type of relationship. All of them had life goals and none of them included her. Dave was attentive and protected her with his life, so no wonder she'd become enchanted by him. Yeah, that was the perfect word, *enchanted*. He'd cast a spell over her, that's for sure. They argued but the banter between them was never cruel. He spoke his mind without holding back and so did she. This was something she found unusual for a military man. They usually acted overly respectful around women. Not that he didn't treat her with respect, but most Marines she'd met had called her ma'am of late and kept their distance. He barked orders at her as if he was above her in the chain of command. She thought on this for a while and looked at him again. He'd neatly folded his cammies and she noted his rank insignia pins were missing from the collar. Why? Perhaps if captured, he'd say he was a deserter or of no consequence to be traded or beheaded for a show on the internet. She frowned, the way he acted and his expertise would denote a high-ranking officer.

Annie kept the fire going by adding wood from a basket piled with logs and added water to the pot and stirred the contents. The sun was high in the sky, and she figured it must be around noon, Dave had slept for four hours and hadn't moved. She stood and stretched, refilled the kettle, and placed it on the fire. She smiled at the ingenious way the grate had been designed. A hook to hang a pot that reminded her of a witch's cauldron and below in the embers sat two smaller iron stands for a kettle and another small pot. She stood and went to the window keeping well behind the blinds. Children kicked a soccer ball in the street and a few people walked along the sidewalk. The town had sustained substantial damage. Many homes stood in ruins. The rows of houses had empty gaping holes like missing teeth. Bombings had destroyed a once thriving town.

She didn't hear Dave get up and dress. He moved like a ghost, not making a sound. When he cleared his throat behind her, it startled her and she spun around to look at him. "Oh, you're awake. Coffee?"

"Sure." He stretched and pressed his hands flat on the ceiling. "It's cramped in here but we'll be moving as soon as it's dark." He took the cup she offered him and sat down at the table, turning the cup in his long fingers. "It's going to be as boring as hell for the next few days but you'll have to be patient. Rest up and get strong. We're

Annie rested her head against his shoulder and held on to him. He felt so good in her arms she didn't want to let go. "Are you really that good? Is that why my dad asked you to rescue me?"

"Let's hope you never have to find out." He brushed a kiss over her lips before stepping back and then gathered up the damp washing and carried it back to the fire. "They've given us goat's milk, sugar, more bread, and *basbousa*." He grinned at her over one shoulder. "I love cream and sugar in my coffee but goat's milk will do just fine."

Suddenly breathless, Annie pressed her fingers to her lips. His kiss had been so gentle and undemanding, but what did it mean? Confused, she hung the towel on the rail and followed him back into the other room. Against the wall, someone had stacked bags and a cardboard box sat on the table. She stared at him. "What's *basbousa*?"

"It's a traditional Middle Eastern semolina cake. It's wonderful, all sweet and sticky. You'll love it." Dave turned to look at the pot on the stove. "Have you been stirring the pot?"

"Yeah." Annie peered in the box and then made the coffee, adding milk and sugar. "It needs water every so often to stop it sticking to the bottom of the pan. "Cake and coffee will be great for lunch. I'm not sure I could eat that casserole or whatever they call it three times a day." She sat down, feeling drained and sore all over. "I'll eat, grab some more pain relief, and then sleep some if that's okay?"

"Sure." Dave pulled the cake from the box and cut it with a knife. "We'll be moving as soon as it gets dark. Once we're at the new safe house, I'll be leaving you alone for maybe a couple of hours. I'll leave a weapon with you and I'd suggest you remain covered until I return. As before, say nothing, keep your eyes on the floor."

Fear dropped over her and she clutched her hands together so he couldn't see them trembling. She swallowed hard. Asking questions seemed taboo but she needed to know. "Where are you going?"

CHAPTER FIFTEEN

Texas

Blood pressure rising, Wolfe stared at the screen array on his desk. In order to gain the locals' cooperation, his operative had sent himself on a suicide mission. His last communication had rocked him to the core. Without anyone to watch his back, Ninety-eight H had set up on the roof of a building, his sniper rifle aimed at the patrolling militia. He chewed on the inside of his mouth as the infrared images moved across the screen. How his operative had organized a group of friendlies to do a cleanup operation in the short time since he'd arrived amazed him, but hadn't made the mission any less dangerous.

Communication with a sniper during a mission was usually restricted to the basic order to proceed or not. A spotter would feed him information about wind and weather and check any other distractions that could alter the trajectory of the bullet. Ninety-eight H was on his own, although his rifle had so many gizmos that he really didn't need a spotter. A sniper needed to use all his powers of concentration, especially at night, to make a clean shot. They usually only took one shot, but with many targets in a combat situation, his sniper would need to be fully engaged to reload and shoot. Wolfe didn't want to distract him, but as his only ally, he had no choice. He pressed his com. "Ninety-eight H, do you copy?"

"Copy."

Wolfe bit back a sigh of relief. "I have you on satellite. Truck with gunner, east of your position, two streets back, moving at ten miles per hour. There's a group of ten or twelve men moving around the building identified as the hostiles' HQ. Foot patrols move out in twos but only move along the perimeter. What do you need from me?"

"Copy. Intel says two trucks patrol at night. Cleanup crews are standing by. Give me a countdown to contact with the patrol. Once we're done here, I'll be moving across town to neutralize the other truck. I figure once the trucks fail to return to base, they'll send out foot patrols. Keep me updated on all movements and countdown to arrival as before. I'll report each downed target."

Wolfe's heart rate increased as the truck slowly rounded the corner. "Copy. Engage truck in twenty seconds." Eyes fixed on the screen, he went silent. Ninety-eight H would be counting down in his head. Heat flared on his sniper's rifle, and the truck veered off the road. Two more flares and then Ninety-eight H came through his earpiece.

"Target down."

In seconds, Ninety-eight H was moving, running across the rooftops. Jumping from building to building. He vanished from sight and his tracker popped up inside a sedan speeding out of a backstreet and weaving between roads across town. On the ground, people moved around the truck, dragging out the driver and passenger and tossing them in the back before it sped off toward the outskirts of town.

Wolfe scanned the screen, following the sedan through the backstreets. He spotted the second militant patrol truck ahead and Ninety-eight H would run straight into it. "Ninety-eight H, do you copy? Second truck dead ahead, change direction. Repeat change direction."

"Copy. Direct to clock tower, town center."

Unease slid over Wolfe. A foot patrol moved along a backstreet only yards from the clock tower. Ninety-eight H would be seen moving from his vehicle carrying such a distinctive weapon. He searched for an alternative route and engaged his com. "Ninety-eight H, do you copy?"

"Copy."

Wolfe swallowed hard. One small mistake and militants would capture, torture, and behead his operative. He sucked in a breath. "Turn left at the next intersection. Suggest shelter in damaged building. Foot patrol moving in from one hundred yards, two men, automatic rifles. Wait until they pass then move through the alleyway and turn left. The clock tower is straight ahead and the way is clear."

"Copy."

Wolfe heaved a sigh of relief as Ninety-eight H ran from the sedan and slid into the building. "I'll keep radio silence until you're in position and then update you with the militia's movements."

"Copy."

Wolfe pushed a hand through his hair to find it damp with sweat although it was cool in his office. He blew out a breath and rubbed his hands down his face. He could see where Ninety-eight H was, but where the hell was Annie?

CHAPTER SIXTEEN

Syria

After listening intently and scanning the immediate area, Dave ran across the road, avoiding the broken bricks and other debris spilling from the ruins of the buildings. With his mind running through possible scenarios, Dave's head was in mission mode. Cool and calm, with every possible outcome considered, he eased inside the shell of the building, his night goggles slightly distorting his view. He left his rifle behind a pile of broken bricks and removed his goggles and placed them beside it, and then moved back to the front of the building. He wore his cammies, and the desert colors blended into the sandy-colored building, making him invisible in the dark and distorted shadows. He stood, arms loose and relaxed at his sides, ready to fight. Using a weapon would alert the neighborhood to his presence. He could take down two untrained men with one arm tied behind his back. The two heavily armed militiamen came into view, walking at a slow pace and occasionally checking the gutted buildings, as if performing a perfunctory task rather than clearing the area.

Dave moved to the other side of the building, to an empty space, and waited. As the men walked past, he tossed a small pebble into the street some ways ahead and another into the darkness surrounding him. As he'd suspected, the two men twisted and turned, unsure of which way to go. Untrained in maneuvers, they made the mistake of splitting up, one going ahead and the other walking straight past him before switching on a flashlight. Before the man swept the room with the beam, Dave attacked. In seconds, his hands wrapped around greasy unwashed hair in a headlock, and before the man uttered a sound, he lay dead at his feet. He stripped him of his weapons, dragged him into the shadows, and waited. In minutes the other man came strolling back toward him.

"Qasim." The man slowed, waving his flashlight from side to side. "What's taking so long? Are you catching a rat for dinner?" He walked past Dave and into the ruins.

No thoughts passed through Dave's mind as he dispatched the second man. He didn't know his name and didn't care. It wasn't as if he kept a tally. That would be too gross. He peered both ways down the street but had no idea if any more militia prowled the streets. He glanced at the two men. The people in town would be safer for his actions. After collecting the rifles, he slung them over one shoulder and went to collect his rifle and night goggles. Next, the second truck and whoever came after it. He touched his com. "Two targets down. Moving to the clock tower."

"Copy that. You're clear but I see people in the houses, close by. They look like women hiding huddled together."

Dave snorted. "I've learned not to trust anyone out here. If anyone heads this way, tell me."

He hustled across the courtyard and into the clock tower. He put down his rifle and looked around. Steps led into darkness. He'd need a position up top with a three-sixty-degree view. When something came hurtling out of a doorway, he spun around ready to fight. He glanced down to see the terrified eyes of a young boy. He took a few steps back. If the kid was rigged with a vest filled with explosives, he'd be a goner. "Open your coat."

The boy complied, turning all around exposing bare flesh. Dave removed his night goggles so as not to frighten the kid. "Why are you here?"

"I'm to take a message to Farid to tell him when you need him to come." His head nodded like a bobblehead. "I will be your lookout."

Dave shook his head. "No, it's not safe. What's your name?"

"Saad." The boy looked up at him and blinked. "I am brave and reliable like my father."

Looking around for a safe place for the boy to hide, Dave indicated to a house across the way. "Is that your house?"

"Yes." The boy looked behind him.

Dave patted him on the shoulder. "Take these weapons and remain inside. When it is over, I'll come for you and you can take me to Farid. Right now, it's not safe for you here." He slid a rifle over each of the boy's shoulders. "Go now and protect your family."

The boy moved slowly under the weight of the rifles. Dave tapped his com. "Any more surprises?"

"Nope, I saw him same time as you. He must have been close to the fire and it hid his heat signature." Terabyte sounded concerned. *"Three women in the house he entered. I can't see anyone close by. The militia truck has been circling the block to the north of your position. It's moving in your direction now. Once it hits the straightaway, it will be in sight of the militia HQ. Once you hit it, it will be like disturbing a bees' nest."*

"Copy. That's the plan. I'm heading upstairs now." Dave picked up his rifle and ran up the stairs taking them two at a time. The tower was as he'd expected, the clock sat in the middle with a walkway around it. Thick brick walls with gaps in between made up a viewing platform for the entire town. Using his scope, he scanned the town to the north until he picked up the headlights of the militia truck. It was the same setup as before. One gunner and two men inside. The truck was heading in his direction through a heavily damaged area on a straight road. Using night goggles, he could make out the men inside the truck and the gunner as if they were a few meters away. He set up his rifle, checked the wind, and dropped into the zone. He'd need three shots, each bullet loaded individually and at top speed. He'd made more complicated shots before over a greater distance. Taking a deep breath, he squeezed the trigger, and before the bullet had reached its target he'd reloaded and fired again. By the time, the truck had veered off the road, mounted the curb, and stopped, he'd taken out the passenger.

The expected fallout was immediate. Heavily armed militia spilled from the HQ. All of them running toward the truck, shooting at random. The sound of loud voices and rapid fire echoed through the town but the streets were empty. The people had taken cover. Dave pressed his com. "How many?"

"Eight. None inside."

As the smell of gunpowder drifted toward him in a cloud, Dave remained in his calm place. He had all the time in the world and recalibrated his rifle and took aim. The distance was an easy shot for him. The only problem was reloading his rifle. The *phut* as each bullet left the muzzle and flew through the air to the targets made hardly a sound. He counted the hits, and pressed his com. "All targets down. Are we clear?"

"Copy that. You're clear to go. There are locals running into the street. It must be the cleanup crew. I suggest you head out of Dodge. Your bounty has just gone through the roof."

Dave smiled as he stripped down his rifle and stowed it in his backpack. "Copy that. I'll go get my ride and the package. We're leaving tonight. The scuttlebutt on the street says there's something big going down in the next twenty-four and as soon as the militia discover I've neutralized their home base, it's going to get hot here real fast. I'll head for the border now. Follow my progress. We'll need an evac ASAP."

"Copy that. Stay safe out there."

Dave headed down the steps and vanished into the night. "I intend to."

CHAPTER SEVENTEEN

The new safe house was a dump. Annie sat on a rickety chair, with the Glock resting on her thigh, staring at the door. Her heart missed a beat with every sound and there were many. People seemed to be close by and she could hear low voices through the walls. It was as if everyone was hiding. A woman had arrived before Dave had left. She'd said nothing but left a pot of the hot sweet yellow coffee, bread, and cheese. They'd eaten everything and then after checking his watch, Dave had left. Since then, she hadn't moved.

When a knock came on the door, heart pounding, she aimed her weapon, holding it high with both hands. She could hear men's voices, low and conspiratorial. Terror had her by the throat but she kept her hands steady with the gun aimed chest high. Footsteps moved away but she heard a scratching on the wall beside the door.

"Annie." Dave's voice was just above a whisper but she recognized it. "Time to go. Unlock the door, I'm alone."

Relieved but not stupid, she hurried to the door, unlocked it, and stood to one side, Glock at the ready, just in case. The door swung open and Dave peeked around it and smiled at her. She lowered her weapon and hugged him close. "Thank God you're safe."

"Thank God you're cautious." Dave smiled down at her and nuzzled her neck.

Annie reluctantly dropped her arms and handed him the Glock. "I was worried sick about you."

"That would be a first." Dave gave her a long look. "I kinda like that someone cares about me." He moved the bags to the door. "If you need to use the bathroom, go now. I'm not planning on stopping until we cross the border."

Annie rubbed her sore back. "Are you tying your backpack onto me again?"

"Yeah, sorry. It's just in case we meet a roadblock. But we'll be moving fast without headlights once we leave the town." He twirled his fingers. "It won't be so heavy. I'll carry most of the ammo, but we'll need to hide the US bills as well."

Annie frowned at him. "What about the drugs? There's no way I'm carrying them through customs." She pulled off her dress and he fitted the backpack.

"We won't be going through customs. We'll have an uncomfortable ride in whatever military vehicle is available but I'll take charge of the backpack. Once we land, we'll be straight into debriefings. They'll want to make sure you haven't been corrupted. The brick of drugs is what I'm using to pay for our vehicle. I'm not taking it back to the States." Dave tightened the straps. "I know this is heavy but you'll be in the vehicle most of the time. We may have to sprint to the chopper, but I'll carry you if necessary."

Annie grabbed her dress and pulled it over her head, surprised when he helped her. She adjusted her burka and met his gaze. "Thanks. Do you need anything before we go? The yellow coffee is lukewarm. I covered the pot to keep it warm for you."

"Yeah, it will help to keep me awake." He pulled the towel from the pot and drank down the fluid and dropped the empty pot onto the table. He dressed hurriedly in his long robes and head covering and then looked her over. "Okay, let's go. Farid said he'd be here in five and it's way past that now. We'll need to move fast before they find out I took out the militia." He picked up the bags and slung them over one shoulder. "Stay close."

Terrified at what might happen next, Annie hurried behind him down the stairs, trying to keep from toppling forward under the weight of the backpack strapped to the front of her. She gripped the handrail but underfoot the way was rough and loose pebbles slid under her boots. Dave moved in silence, not even his boots crunched on the gravel as they reached the sidewalk. She couldn't see the vehicle pulling up to the curb as Dave had his entire body blocking her from view. After a rapid exchange in Arabic, Dave handed over the drugs. She assumed by the jangle it was in exchange for a set of keys. She came out from behind him and his fingers closed around her arm as he propelled her toward a battered four-by-four. Bullet holes riddled one side but she noticed two gas cans in the back and what looked like a plastic container carrying about two gallons of water. She climbed inside, holding the backpack, and dropping the weight between her legs before stretching the seatbelt around her and clipping it in place.

"Hold on to anything you can find." Dave slid in behind the wheel and they took off at full speed. He didn't take his eyes off the road as he handed her a map and flashlight. "You're the navigator. Take the map, the route is marked, the cross is where we are now. Only use the flashlight in short bursts when checking the map. We don't need to be seen." He glanced at her as she stared at the map. "Turn it the other way up. You can read a map, can't you?"

Annie's face grew hot. She'd always relied on her GPS or phone. "I'll do my best but everything is in Arabic."

"Roads are roads, crossroads the same." Dave glanced at the map and made a sharp left turn and headed down a long narrow road. He dug a finger into the map. "This is the road we're on now, follow the red pen line, tell me to turn left or right at the intersections. Got it?

Count the roads ahead of the next turn. So, say, in five blocks, tell me to turn left. Understand?"

Wishing he'd just keep his eyes on the road, Annie gripped on to the seat with one hand and stared at the map. Looking ahead as side roads flashed past, too fast to keep count, she gave up on that idea as a bad joke and glanced at him. "Right turn next intersection, then a sharp left, go through a town square, and then straight ahead."

"Copy." Dave slammed his foot on the gas and the truck sped through the night. "Once we get out of the town, I'll use my night goggles and kill the lights. I'll be able to see fine. I know there's only one or two main highways to the border. I'll be in contact with my handler and he'll be guiding me from there." He flashed her a white smile. "You're doing fine."

They dashed through the town square and the truck bumped and slid on the gravel as they made the turns. Heart in her mouth and her fingers white-knuckling the seat, she waited until they hit the straightaway and glanced again at the map. "This road veers to the left up ahead. You'll need to slow down to make a left, then straight ahead and another left. We go under a bridge, then there's a straight run out of suburbia. From there it's just one road as far as I can make out."

"Copy that." Dave changed gears up and down, braking hard and then taking off, leaving a shower of dust and rocks behind them.

As they raced through mostly ruins, she noticed a few low-burning lights but it seemed most of the people were either hiding or in bed asleep. As they left the town behind them, Dave pulled on his night-vision goggles and killed the lights. Annie gripped the seat and side of the truck so hard her hands ached. She could hardly make out Dave's outline in the dark, but she could see his jaw set in concentration and his eyes fixed on the road. He was fearless and they sped into the black night like a rocket through space.

The bumps in the road scared the life out of her. The truck would hit a pothole and buck and slide, throwing her this way and that, but somehow, Dave kept the vehicle on the road. He said nothing, his concentration taken up with driving. Mile after mile of blackness flashed by. She could see the stars, so close she could almost touch them, but out here was barren sandy soil and nothing for miles and miles. She'd listened with interest to the conversation between Dave and a contact he called Terabyte. She understood the need for code names and from Dave's limited side of the conversation, she gained nothing, as his replies were no more than "copy." So after an hour's silence, Dave's voice surprised her.

"What did you do at the embassy?" Dave flicked her a glance.

Annie smiled at him. "If I told you, I'd have to kill you." She watched his mouth twitch at the corners. "That's the correct reply, isn't it?'

"Let me rephrase that." Dave swerved to avoid a pothole in the road. "What are you planning on doing when you return home? When all this is over, I'd like to come and visit you. If you want me to?"

Annie tried to relax her aching jaw to ease the pain. She'd been grinding her teeth the entire trip. "I'd like that. I worked at the embassy to get wider experience, but I applied for a position as a secretary to a family court magistrate in DC, and I'll be able to start there in a month or so. His current secretary is leaving as she's expecting a baby. She has three kids already and wants to devote more time to her family." She sighed. "She's a friend of the family and recommended me. I have an undergraduate degree in family law and plan to return to my studies. This position offers me that chance." She turned to look at him. "What about you?"

"I go where they send me." Dave shrugged. "I don't have the option of making choices at the moment. I'm hoping in a few months maybe I'll be offered a desk job." He snorted. "I won't be happy behind a desk but it beats being out here."

"It must be lonely out there." Annie frowned. "I do have some idea of the life of a sniper. Why did you pick that area of expertise? You must have known how dangerous it would be."

"Someone has to do it and I'm damn good at what I do. I can't say that I get lonely because I'm never really alone." Dave shrugged. "There's always someone in my ear." He cleared his throat. "Like now." He pressed his ear and listened for a few moments. "Copy." He glanced at her. "Hide these."

Fear gripped her as Dave ripped off his night-vision goggles and tossed them to her. She lifted her dress and slid them into his backpack. When he flicked on the headlights as the road ahead rounded a huge hill, she noticed the tic in the nerve in his cheek. Something was terribly wrong. "What is it?"

"There's a patrol just up ahead. They'll be the first line of militia guarding the border. It's only a mile or so from here." He pulled out his sidearm and rested it on his knee under his robe. "Have the Glock ready. I'll say you're in labor and they might allow us to pass. We don't have any papers. If they order us out of the vehicle, we'll have to fight. If we survive, the chopper is standing by just over the border and will risk an evac once we deal with the militia."

Fingers trembling, Annie pulled the Glock from the pocket in her dress, chambered a bullet, and held it under the folds of her dress beside her on the seat. They rounded the corner. Across the road two trucks blocked the way and as they approached five men appeared in the headlights. Beside her, Dave seemed to relax, the opposite to her, and calmly pressed his earpiece concealed under his headgear.

"I see five, is that all…? Copy." Dave turned to look at her as the car slowed. "Moaning is good, and clutching your belly. You know the deal, right?" He wet his lips. "If it all goes to hell, I'll take them out."

Annie gaped at him. "Five of them? Have you lost your mind?"

"Well, you can help if you like but you'll probably get yourself killed by drawing their fire." He slowed the truck. "Eyes down, don't look at these guys or we're dead for sure."

Rigid with fear, Annie moaned and held her belly, leaning forward in the seat helped to keep her eyes covered. Beside her, Dave waved his arms and from his tone, he was ordering the men to allow them to pass. The men moved closer and peered inside. They must have been demanding papers because they raised their weapons. Dave slid from behind the wheel, arguing all the time and then one of the men walked up to the vehicle and pulled open her door. One of his hands went around her arm and another stroked her thigh. Without a second thought, Annie lifted the Glock to his face.

The sound of the weapon discharging deafened her. Rapid gunfire came from beside her and she turned as Dave shot two of the men and then ducked behind the truck. The other two men scattered, taking up positions behind their vehicles, and bullets pinged off the metal all around her. She ducked down, lying across the seats as the windshield smashed, and a bullet thudded into the seat beside her head. Keeping low, she slid out of the vehicle, stepped over the dead man, and headed back to where Dave was returning fire. Over the noise she could hear him talking and then the *whoop whoop* of a chopper came from above. Bright lights searched the area and the chopper's guns fired a thousand bullets into the militia truck, but the men still returned fire.

"Run to the chopper, Annie." Dave was beside her. "I'll be right behind you."

Terrified, Annie ran. The weight of the heavy bag didn't register. Adrenalin was pumping so fast through her veins she'd turned into a superhero. Bullets zinged past her and just as Dave lifted her and threw her into the chopper, something grazed her cheek. He fell in the door and landed on top of her, pinning her to the floor. Wind buffeted around them. The sides of the chopper had no doors, just big gaping holes. The next moment Dave rolled off her and a navy Seal dragged her into a seat and strapped her in. Annie couldn't hear a thing. The ringing in her ears and the noise of the chopper cut out everything. She stared at Dave, but he just lay on his back on the floor breathing heavily as the chopper gained height. Hands trembling, she glanced down, realizing she was still clinging to the Glock and gaped at the blood splattering her clothes. She closed her eyes, trying to block out the flashes of what had happened. It was as if her mind needed to relive each terrible moment. *I killed a man.*

*

The trip was short and they soon landed on a runway. She made out US military uniforms and started to breathe again. They'd made it to Turkey and the next stop would be home. Outside the chopper Dave pulled off his disguise, and Annie gasped in horror at his blood-soaked shirt as they ran to the open door of a massive military aircraft. Inside stood a row of large boxes covered by nets. The smell of a machinery warehouse engulfed her. The engine roared into life, vibrating through the plane. To her left, a few men in uniform sat on uncomfortable-looking seats against the wall. She mouthed to him, "Are you okay?" but he just urged her into a seat and strapped her in. As the huge door closed and the aircraft took to the sky, she turned to look at him and pointed to his chest. "You're bleeding."

"I'm okay. It's a through-and-through." After the plane evened out, he unbuckled his restraint and then hers. He offered her his hand. "I'll need my backpack. I'll help you out of the dress. You're well covered and those men wouldn't dare to look at you." He pulled her to her feet and had the backpack removed and a blanket wrapped around her in seconds. "I'll go grab a med kit." He wandered off deep into the plane.

The men strapped in a few seats down started mumbling under their breath but sat eyes front when Dave returned sometime later in a clean shirt. Annie noticed he'd replaced his rank pins in his collar.

"Remove the burka. You have blood on you too. Is any of it yours?" Dave dropped another blanket to her and unclasped her harness. He hunched down beside her and narrowed his gaze. "It looks like the bullet went through me and grazed your chin." He opened the med kit and went to work cleaning her up. "It will be fine." He pressed a dressing to her chin. "A doctor will check it when we land."

Horrified, Annie gaped at the blood seeping through the shoulder of his shirt and couldn't imagine the pain he was suffering. "What about you? You're still bleeding."

"I'll be fine." Dave frowned at her as if surprised by her concern. "One of the guys fixed me up."

Annie sat back down and fastened the harness. As realization dawned on her, she turned to him. "You took a bullet for me and saved my life. How can I ever repay you?"

"Just doing my job." Dave looked at her. "But I'll take the coffee you offered to buy me, next time I'm in town."

"I'll look forward to it and I'll be waiting." Taken aback by the sudden flash of his smile, Annie leaned closer and kissed him. When he kissed her back, everything inside her melted. She sighed when he broke the kiss and leaned back. "How will I find you? I don't even know your name."

"I'll find you, I promise." Dave touched her cheek.

She couldn't lose him, not after all they'd been through. "What happens now?"

"For me? A darn lot of paperwork and debriefing. As soon as the wound has healed, they'll send me back in." He leaned back and closed his eyes. "Get some shut-eye. It's going to be a long time before we touch down. Don't worry, they'll let your dad know you're safe. He'll be waiting for you when we arrive."

Annie leaned back but her gaze rested on him, the handsome stranger who'd risked his life to save her countless times. He could be killed on his next mission and she'd never know what happened to him. Heck, she didn't even know his real name.

CHAPTER EIGHTEEN

Washington, DC

Two years later

As Dave stood to one side of the stage as POTUS gave a speech, he listened to the chatter through his earpiece and reflected on his time in the Middle East. He'd yet to find Annie and take her up on the offer of a coffee, but after so long, he'd likely become a distant memory. Such was his life of late. His debriefing on his return had been illuminating in more ways than one. He'd discovered a terrorist organization in Syria had placed a bounty on his head and had spread his photograph all over their media. The risk to continue as a sniper was too great, and they wanted him to remain Stateside until things cooled down but he'd refused the offer of a desk job. It would have killed him with boredom. He'd turned to his handler for guidance. Terabyte, a man he'd never met but whom he trusted with his life, knew him better than anyone. His advice was to do something he enjoyed. Dave had mentioned his interest in investigating crimes of every description but didn't really want to join the FBI. That path was always an option. With his skill set and numerous degrees, he'd walk into a position after a short course of study.

The problem was he'd become too much of a loner. He didn't mind traveling and had no one to come home to apart from his sister, Josie. Divorced, without kids, and a genius, she'd become a professor at Georgetown University at twenty-two. Due to his busy lifestyle, they only spoke on birthdays and holidays. Taking all this into consideration, Terabyte had suggested the Secret Service. Dave liked the idea. It covered a wide variety of skills and opportunities. Strangely, after speaking with Terabyte, within a week, he'd been summoned back to the Oval Office. Dave hadn't been overly worried. POTUS had awarded him a medal for rescuing Annie, so he couldn't have done anything to upset anyone and he'd known the president since he'd been a kid. His father had been POTUS's best man at his wedding and they'd been close family friends until his parents died. Although apart from Christmas and birthday cards, usually from his wife, the man who'd become president hadn't interfered with his life—until that day.

Dave had listened in stunned silence as POTUS informed him of his promise to his father. If anything should happen to Dave's father, POTUS would watch over him and his sister. Although the president understood that as the son of a two-star, Dave wanted to prove his worth without help, he'd stood aside and allowed him to make his own way in the world without assistance. But now, with a bounty on his head, he wanted him close, fearing retribution even on home ground. POTUS had echoed Terabyte's suggestion to become a Secret Service agent. Dave agreed and headed down to the Federal Law Enforcement Training Centers based in Glynco, Georgia, to complete a ten-week Criminal Investigator Training Program. After completion, he returned to Washington, DC, to complete a seventeen-week special agent training course at the James J. Rowley Training Center. He'd returned with his black suit and sunglasses, feeling like a fish out of water, straight into the role of personal protection for POTUS and as an unusual crimes investigator, the latter he enjoyed.

The most significant thing that happened during his second talk with POTUS was the revelation his father had left him a fortune in an offshore bank account. He'd inherited the family house, and both he and his sister had more than they'd ever need from the inheritance from his grandparents and the life insurance policies of his parents. However, his grandfather had shares in mining companies worldwide, and due to a disagreement, his father had refused to accept the lucrative dividends. Instead, he'd set up an offshore bank account in Dave's name. It had been left to accumulate on the off chance, due to Dave's activities on behalf of the government, he might need to disappear one day. Now with a bounty on his head, the day could be soon or never, but a failsafe had been activated. He would retain Terabyte as his handler, who, if necessary, had the contacts to obtain all the assistance he required. If in the future Dave needed to vanish, his handler could obtain passports in various names and had cash stashed in safety deposit boxes in banks all over. The offshore account, set up as a company, could be used to transfer funds without undue suspicion. Such were the dangerous times he lived in.

Dave scanned the room behind his shades. He used to think they were part of the costume or whatever, but often with the glare of the lights he needed to see everyone in all areas of the room. Agents had been posted everywhere and he'd been in constant contact with them during the speech. One of his colleagues had requested an urgent visit to the bathroom and Dave moved into a better position, closer to POTUS, to cover the missing man. He'd been in communication with the other men, constantly checking any possible threats throughout the speech. One thing that the instructors had drummed into them during training was to deactivate their com if they needed some personal time. Needless to say, the man in the bathroom shouldn't have eaten the shrimp.

Dave glanced over at his colleague's twitching lips and smothered a grin. Laughing during POTUS's speech was not part of his job description. He scanned the crowd again and his eyes settled on someone very familiar, and she was looking straight back at him. Annie Parkes stood out in the crowd like a shining beacon. Dressed in a neat business suit with her long hair hanging over her shoulders, she was a distraction. He dragged his eyes away from her and swept the room again, but as his gaze moved over her again, there she was smiling broadly at him. She held up her hand mimicking a cup and sipped. He gave her an imperceivable nod and kept on scanning the room. He had a president to protect and his safety was his first priority, but he'd get her number and give her a call. It had been two years, and not a day had gone by that he hadn't thought about their time in Syria and how he'd allowed her to slip from his life. He'd often wondered what Annie Parkes was doing and today was the day he'd find out.

CHAPTER NINETEEN

Excitement tingled through Annie as she stared at Dave standing straight and tall on the stage. The horror of the kidnapping washed over her at the sight of him but the good memories of their time together replaced it in an instant. Seeing him again made her toes curl. Their attraction had been magnetic, but when she'd said goodbye to him, she understood his duty would get in the way of any relationship for some time. But now he was here and it took all her willpower not to run across the room and throw herself into his arms. She couldn't believe she'd just walked into the hall to listen to the president's speech and found him. It was as if her father had asked her to come along because he knew Dave would be there. Maybe he'd relented after her persistent requests to find him, because no amount of coercion had made her father give her any details of what had happened to Dave after their arrival in the US. She'd been bundled into her father's sedan and whisked away to a hospital, where she'd undergone so many tests, both mental and physical, she didn't know what day it was. Each time she'd asked how Dave was doing, she got a stony blank stare. Of course, no one had any idea who Dave was, but she hadn't given up, and devised a plan of sorts to find her elusive rescuer.

After leaving the hospital, she decided to visit her father's office when he wouldn't be there. She'd checked his diary and found he would be attending a meeting. She'd insisted his desk sergeant put a call through to the command center and offered to take full responsibility for disturbing her father. She'd gone into his office, picked up his phone, and waited for the switchboard to answer. "This is General Parkes' office. Connect me with Terabyte."

"Copy, is there a problem, General?" A Texas drawl came down the line.

Annie swallowed hard; this was breaking every rule in the book. "This is Annie Parkes. I know you're the handler for the man who rescued me. I call him Dave. Is there any way I can get in contact with him? Is he okay? He took a bullet for me. I owe him my life."

"Ma'am, as the daughter of a three-star, you know I'm not at liberty to give you any information." Terabyte sounded stiff and cautious.

Annie let out a cry of frustration. "I know he speaks to you. Look, fine, don't tell me anything, but let him know the coffee offer is still on the table and will remain there."

"Copy. But I can't guarantee he'll get the message. I don't have the authority to pass on messages to him, but I'll do my best." The line went dead.

That had been two years ago. Although she had to admit for a while there that she'd attended functions with her father in the hope she'd see Dave in the crowd, but it was as if he'd vanished. He'd almost faded from her memory and then the moment she'd set eyes on him again, out of the blue, all her feelings had come rushing back. Now he was standing a few yards from her, as large as life and twice as handsome. She couldn't stop staring at him but he made no contact with her at all. The slight nod he gave her was the only indication he'd recognized her. Now what could she do? As a Secret Service agent, he'd be glued to POTUS right up to the time they reached the safety of the White House. She looked around the room, seeing the other agents spread out all noticeable in their suits and earwigs. She took out one of her cards and wrote a note on the back: *I owe you a coffee.*

Approaching a Secret Service agent on duty was probably like poking a lion but throwing caution to the wind, she wandered up to the closest Secret Service agent and stood beside him. She knew all about their open coms and raised her voice. "Dave, I'm leaving my card with the tall blond agent. Call me."

Holding her breath, Annie watched Dave scan the room and rest on her for a millisecond before moving away. He'd heard her. She smiled at the blond agent, who'd not as much as registered her presence, and pushed her card into his top pocket. "Give my card to the big guy on the stage." She turned away and eased through the crowd and out the room.

Leaning against the cool marble wall in the hallway, she tried to slow her racing heart. She glanced at her watch. It was a little after eight. She slipped out of the building, ran to the parking lot, and jumped into her Ford. In ten minutes, she'd arrived at her small apartment overlooking the Potomac. She showered and changed into casual clothes. Would he call?

Not hungry but needing something to occupy her mind, she filled the coffee pot, made a ham on rye sandwich, and sat in front of the TV. But her mind wasn't on the program, it was stuck on Dave, as if she'd superimposed the image of him on her brain. She couldn't stop smiling. She'd found him. He worked for the Secret Service. She sighed as the time dragged by. The ball was in his court now. She rubbed her arms. He could be married and the slight nod might have just been recognition, not anything else.

After talking herself out of the possibilities of him calling her, her phone chimed just after ten. She grabbed it up and accepted the call. "Hello."

"I was surprised to see you." Dave's voice filled her head. *"You know obstructing a federal agent in the course of his duty is an offense?"*

Annie giggled. "It was worth the risk to hear your voice again. I've been trying to find you. I have a debt to repay."

"No, you don't." Dave sounded serious again. *"I was just following orders is all."*

Annie let out an exasperated sigh. "Oh, for heaven's sake, Dave. It's just a coffee, but unless you're married or involved with someone and meeting up will cause a problem, the invitation is still on the table."

"Uh-huh." Dave sounded highly amused. *"I'm not involved with anyone, but thanks for asking. Are you? I'm a little old-fashioned about meeting up with married women."*

"No, not at the moment." Annie chuckled. "So, are we on?"

"Yeah, I'd love a coffee." Dave sounded so relaxed.

Wanting to squeal with delight, Annie took a deep breath. "When and where?"

"I'm outside your building, buzz me up." Dave cleared his throat. *"You do have a coffee machine? I've never been able to drink instant coffee since returning to the States."*

Dashing across the room, Annie pressed the door release beside the intercom. "I sure do. Sixth floor, the apartment opposite the elevator."

"Oh, I know where you live. Once you gave me your phone number, I traced you. I wasn't planning on you vanishing twice." Dave chuckled and the line went dead.

Annie dashed into the bathroom to brush her hair and add a little perfume. The knock came on the door seconds after. She opened the door and stared at him. No longer in his black suit, he'd dressed in a dark blue sweater that matched his eyes and black jeans. He was taller and broader than she'd remembered and not so tanned. His hair looked darker, no longer in a buzz cut, but fashionable, and he looked relaxed and at peace. She must have been ogling him for some time because he gave her a slow smile. Heat rushed to her cheeks and she stepped to one side. "Hi, Dave. Come in. It's so good to see you. What took you so long to find me? It's been two long years, you know?"

"Hi, Annie. If I'd had your number, I'd have contacted you the moment I came home, but I wouldn't have been able to see you before now anyway. POTUS hasn't given me five minutes to myself since returning to the States." He stepped inside and looked at her, his eyes dancing with amusement. "You sure look good, Annie. I couldn't believe it was you in the crowd. I'm back in DC for good now." His gaze scanned her face. "After two years, I thought you'd have forgotten me. I'm sure glad you didn't."

Annie laughed. "You're not someone I could forget in a hurry, Dave. I asked around to see if you were okay when we got back, but Terabyte shut me down."

"Yeah, he does that." His gaze drifted over her. "You're even lovelier than I remember."

The electricity between them sizzled and, without thinking, Annie reached up, cupped his cheek, and looked into his eyes. He smelled so good it made her glow all over. When his arms came around her it was as if she'd known him all her life. This was where she belonged and coffee was the last thing on her mind.

CHAPTER TWENTY

Six months later

Winter had come as usual with freezing temperatures and snow, but the entire world could freeze over and it couldn't cool Dave's love of Annie. She was the dream he'd never dared to imagine, the life he'd never thought possible. He wanted to marry Annie and had already purchased a set of rings, but he understood the risk involved. Before he asked her, he wanted to speak to her father to make sure he wouldn't be called back to active duty. His work had become more involved of late, his time taken up with solving many types of crime. He often traveled to investigate, but POTUS still had his finger in the pie of his life. After so long without retribution from Syrian militants, it had become a little stifling. He couldn't expect Annie to live her life never knowing if he'd come home. Life as a sniper or government assassin, whatever the fancy label, meant being expendable, and given the bounty on his head, his best-by date was closing in fast.

On arrival at General Parkes' office, he waited for some time in the outer office. The room had a strange odor of cigars and stale aftershave. Once inside, he found the general to be formal to the max. Parkes ignored him for some minutes and when he finally raised his small eyes from his computer screen, he didn't ask him to sit. Although inactive, Dave held the rank of colonel, and the general's attitude surprised him. But he remained at ease before his desk. As Dave had never been discharged from service, with a flick of a pen, POTUS could order the general to send him back to the desert with his rifle.

"What can I do for you, Agent?" Parkes' eyebrows drew together in the middle. "I'm not the person you should be speaking to if you have a problem. I'm no longer in your chain of command."

Dave cleared his throat. "You'll be aware I'm seeing Annie?"

"Yes, she never stops talking about you. You must have made a good impression on her in Syria." Parkes gave him a long stare. "She calls you Dave. I imagine you're not revealing your true identity to her by order of POTUS?"

The tightening in his gut came as a warning that Parkes wasn't impressed by him. He nodded. "It's better that no one knows my true identity, for the safety of everyone I work with, sir." He met the general's hard gaze. "This is why I came to speak with you. I love Annie and want to marry her. It's been over two years since Syria, and I figure I'm safe."

"What does Annie say about this?" Parkes leaned back in his chair, twirling a pen in his fingers. "You could be called back into service at any time. You're the best we have, and should the need arise, we might need you again. Would she be happy knowing the chances of your survival on a mission would be negligible?"

Uncomfortable, Dave straightened. "I haven't discussed it with her, but she's aware I might be called back to active duty. I thought it would be better to speak with you before I proposed. I don't want to hurt her by asking her to marry me and then walking away if POTUS needs me."

"You're in love, you say?" Parkes stopped twirling the pen.

"We're in love." Dave smiled. "She means the world to me, but my fear is once we're married, she becomes a target. I'll have to use my real name to legally marry her."

"There is a way to protect her." Parkes dropped the pen into a cup. "If you married in secret and she retained her last name, no one would be the wiser. In fact, we could change your name to Parkes as one of your various identities should you need to travel, but I think traveling overseas might cause undue attention. The name is one thing but you can't change your face—well that is an option, but only in the most extreme cases." He paused, a beat. "I'll do what I can to run interference should POTUS decide to call you back into active service, and we have other superb snipers I can suggest." He smiled. "I do have POTUS's ear in these matters."

Euphoria poured over Dave and he stared at the general in disbelief. "So, we have your blessing?"

"Yes, you do. I'm sure you'll make her very happy." The general stood and offered his hand. "Welcome to the family. I'll get the paperwork underway for her to retain her name and anything else you need. When do you want this to happen?"

What if she doesn't want marriage so soon? Dave swallowed hard. "I guess I should propose first, and if she accepts, I'm sure Annie will decide the date and want a hand in the organization."

"I'm sure she will." The general smiled at him. "Tell her to call me, and we'll get things rolling."

Overwhelmed with joy, Dave grinned. "Thank you, sir." He turned and left the room, his legs feeling a little wobbly for the first time in his life.

CHAPTER TWENTY-ONE

At last it was Friday night, and Dave had asked Annie on a special date. The offer of a meal at her favorite restaurant was a nice surprise. As Dave usually didn't have too much time for a romantic dinner, their relationship had taken a back seat to his work, but he'd spent every second of his downtime with her. Annie understood his workload, but over the past couple of weeks his protection detail had decreased and he'd wound up on a recent investigation into heaven knows what. He never discussed his work, apart from things like having an itchy back or other distractions when standing close to POTUS during a speech. Annie smiled at the memory. They'd laughed so hard, after catching a glimpse of him on the news, standing on an ant's nest with an expression carved in stone, as POTUS planted a tree.

Excited to be going out with him, Annie dressed in a silk shirt under a figure-flattering black wool jacket and skirt. After selecting six-inch heels to accentuate her legs, she'd brushed her hair until it shone and left it loose about her shoulders. She only wore a hint of makeup and added a dab of the Chanel N° 5 he'd given her for her birthday. Her gaze moved to the clock. He'd arrive in a few minutes and she could set her watch by him. Pulling on her thick winter coat and gloves, she slipped her purse over one shoulder and headed for the door. Dave would likely be driving up outside her building by the time she hit the foyer. She waited for the elevator doors to open and rode it down. The doorman gave her a wave from behind the desk as she headed for the glass doors.

Outside, a blast of wind slapped her face and, wrapping her coat tight around her, she peered along the curb. Gray snow piled up along the sidewalk, filled with sticks and leaves, but a good coating of salt was keeping the ice away for now and at least it wasn't snowing. Dave's truck wasn't easy to miss but vehicles crammed the street, making it difficult to make out his truck from a line of dark-colored vehicles. The popularity of the bistro on the next block often caused parking problems, but usually Dave parked in the space under her building. She'd gotten him his own swipe card for her building, which made life easier, but as they had reservations, she'd planned to meet him downstairs. Lights flashed in the line of vehicles and after giving a wave, Annie hurried along the slippery sidewalk. After a few yards she heard footsteps pounding behind her. As they slowed, pain slammed into her head and she tumbled face-first into the bushes. Grabbing hold of the bare sticks, she pushed back and tried to balance on her high heels. The next second someone took hold of her purse and dragged it from her shoulder. A dark figure loomed over her and she tightened her grip on the strap. The smell of bad breath and sweat filled her nostrils and she stared into the wild eyes of a heavily breathing stranger. "Get off me." She swiped at his face.

As his hands closed around her throat, she heard the roar of an engine. It was like a kidnapping rerun, but this time she'd fight back and went for his eyes, digging her thumbs deep just as Dave had taught her. The man screamed and shook her, but suddenly, wasn't there anymore. The weight of him vanished as he flew backward, landing on the sidewalk. The next second he was flat on his face with Dave's knee in his back, his arms bent back almost to his shoulders. As a couple ran to help her, Annie staggered to her feet. The man had rescued her purse and handed it to her. "Thanks, I'll be fine. The big guy is my boyfriend."

"Lucky you." The woman smiled. "We'll wait for the cops. I caught everything on my phone."

Annie brushed the snow off her coat. "Thank you." She turned at Dave's voice.

"Annie." Dave's eyes flashed with anger as he dragged the man back toward her. "Did he hurt you?" He had the man secured with flexicuffs and shoved him hard against a wall. His voice dropped low and menacing as he leaned into the man. "Don't as much as blink."

Shaken and a little bruised, Annie nodded her head. "I'm okay. He grabbed my purse and then tried to strangle me."

"I'll call it in." Dave's gaze moved over her. "You'd better go back inside in the warm. I'll be there in a minute."

Annie shook her head. "I'd rather be out here with you."

She leaned against the wall as Dave made the call, and in a few minutes the blacktop flashed blue and red as it filled with cop cars. A detective spoke to Dave, and when he showed his cred pack, everything went into fast-forward. The moment the man was bundled into a cruiser, Dave came to her side. She leaned into him, as his arms came around her. The expression on his face was one she'd seen in Syria. He'd become remote and distant as if he'd become a robot. She looked up at him. "I'm okay. He was just trying to steal my purse."

"Yeah, I can see that by the bruises on your neck." Dave touched her cheek. "I wanted to tear him apart. Will you be okay? I'll need to speak to the detective again."

Annie gripped his arm. "I know I'll have to give a statement. I guess we'll be missing our dinner?"

"Do you still want to go?" Dave met her gaze. "He tried to kill you."

Annie touched her neck. "We've been through worse than this together. I'm not going to allow that piece of garbage to spoil our night."

"We'll still have time. I booked the table for nine." Dave rubbed her back. "It will be hours before they get to him. It's Friday night and they'll place him in a holding cell until the paperwork is completed. They have eyewitnesses and video footage to process. I'll tell the detective we'll drop by later."

They spoke to the detective, a man in his fifties, his nose red from the cold, and Annie listened to everything he had to say and answered his questions. The man who'd attacked her was known to police and had previous convictions for purse snatching and assault. She noticed the tension ease from Dave's expression on hearing this information. She'd have to get him out of the habit of blaming himself for everything that happened around him. The icy wind cut through her clothes and she just wanted to get warm, but she agreed to allow the paramedics on scene to check her over. Once everyone was satisfied, she climbed into Dave's truck and peered at herself in her compact mirror. She combed her hair and turned to look at him. "My clothes are fine and my neck looks okay. Can we go eat now?"

"Yeah, but my plans are shot to hell." Dave gave her a rueful smile. "I wanted to drop by early and take you to a romantic spot, a place we could keep in our memories." He sighed. "Don't worry, there is another nice place nearby."

Annie's stomach gave a little flip when he drove to a spot alongside the Potomac and parked. The lights of the city looked magical, reflected in the wide river and coloring the recent covering of snow. "That's a beautiful view."

"Mine is better." He took her hand and stared into her eyes. His anger had vanished, replaced by a softness he always had when he looked at her. "You know, since Syria I've had a bounty on my head?"

Suddenly afraid, Annie nodded. "Yeah, but that was over two years ago and nothing has happened. Why?"

"What happened tonight might not have been a purse snatching. It could be someone trying to get to me by hurting you." Dave searched her face. "Honestly, I figure they'd use a professional. But taking all this into consideration and the possible threat to our lives, will you marry me?"

Astonished, Annie stared at him trying to process his words. She couldn't answer and just kissed him and then raised her head. "A million times, yes." She cupped his face. "I know you'll keep me safe, Dave. There is only one thing. Will you tell me your real name?"

When Dave whispered in her ear, she blinked at him. "Like the general?"

"Yeah, he was my dad." Dave shrugged. "Go figure, two general's kids deciding to get married." He laughed. "Your dad suggested we use your last name to keep mine secure. I can take any identity, but we'll have to marry under my real name to make it legal."

Annie looked at him and smiled. "Can I still call you Dave? I think it suits you. Being named after your father must have been terrible growing up?"

"Yeah, well they never used my name; they called me Junior most times." He reached into his pocket. "So, Dave is fine by me and I've gotten used to it. It's our special name." He opened a ring box. "I hope you don't want a long engagement. I've purchased matching sets of wedding rings to go with this."

Annie gaped at an exquisite diamond ring. A simple pear-shaped diamond set in yellow gold. "I'd have been happy with a cigar wrapper." She held out her hand as he slipped it on her finger. "Wow! I love it and I don't want to wait either." She giggled. "How about tomorrow?"

"As soon as we can get things organized, works for me, but I have another confession." Dave pressed kisses to her cheek. "I'm loaded."

Laughing, Annie hugged him. "I have one too. You do know I want a dozen kids?"

"Me too and we'll get a dog. Kids need a dog." Dave let out a long sigh and looked chagrined. "I already asked for your dad's blessing. I didn't want any complications. He figures, because of my past, a secret wedding will be safer. So, if you really don't want to wait, call your dad. He wants to be involved."

Annie laughed. "My dad is a teddy bear, isn't he?" She looked at him. "My parents have a lovely home with a pergola. I'm happy with a marriage celebrant or a trip to Vegas, whenever we can arrange it."

"Okay." He grinned at her. "Let's go and celebrate."

CHAPTER TWENTY-TWO

After dinner, Dave had gotten as far as the elevator in Annie's apartment building on the way from dinner when his phone chimed. "Yeah?"

"This is the dean of Georgetown University. I have your number down as the next of kin contact for Professor Josephine Henley. Am I speaking to Mr. Henley?"

An uneasy feeling crept over Dave. They'd used his sister's married name and assumed they'd contacted her ex-husband. "I'm Josie's brother. Is she okay? What's happened?"

"I'm sorry to call so late, but she was due to drop by this week and we haven't heard from her. The new semester starts on Monday. I've called her cell and home with no response. I became worried, so asked the local police to drop by. They spoke to the neighbors and one of them mentioned she planned to go by your grandparents' house. She'd received a call about a tree down from a storm. It seems so strange she wouldn't return my messages. As she still hasn't called, I thought I should contact you."

Why wouldn't Josie call him about the tree? It was his house. Not that he ever went there. It held too many sad memories. The smell of death still lingered after his grandma died there and being the one to find her at just sixteen years old, hadn't endeared him to the place. He'd planned to sell it long before now. However, because of Josie he'd delayed the sale. She had a habit of visiting the old place, switching off her phone, and just chilling for days without informing anyone. He'd left the power connected and found the supplies she'd left for her visits in the freezer and pantry. Being at the house obviously offered her some comfort in times of stress, but when he'd offered to give her the house she'd refused.

Although the home had passed to his father, Dave's parents hadn't raised their kids there. Like most military brats they'd been raised all over the world, but Josie had often spent summers with their grandparents. Her memories were obviously different from his own. He drew in a deep breath. "Okay, leave it with me. I'll track her down. Thanks for calling." He disconnected.

"What's happened?" Annie gripped his arm.

Dave shook his head. "Maybe nothing. My sister isn't picking up her phone and her work is trying to get in contact with her, so they called me." He sighed. "This isn't unusual for her but I'll try and track her down."

Dave called the local general store close to his grandparent's house. The family had owned the store for as long as he remembered and lived above the store. Josie could have dropped by for supplies or information. The number picked up after a minute or so. "Hi, Mrs. Philibert. I'm really sorry to disturb you so late. This is Junior, the general's son. Remember me?"

"I sure do, Junior, and it's no trouble. We always stay up and watch the movie on Friday nights." The old lady sounded happy to speak to him. *"I was just talking to Josie about the tree that came down in the storm. There's many around here who could make use of the wood."*

Dave smiled to himself. "When did you last speak with her?"

"That would be Thursday morning." Mrs. Philibert paused a beat. *"She's stressed out about something at work and will be staying a few days. She posted a sign in my window to give away the wood. She had the tree service cut it up for her. It must have cost a pretty penny. I told her she should sell it but she'd have none of it. She made up the notice right there and then."*

"Thanks, Mrs. Philibert. I'll drop by tomorrow and give her a hand." Dave disconnected and contacted Terabyte. "My sister has gone AWOL. I'll need a couple of days to go and check if she's okay. I'm on duty this weekend but one of the guys will cover for me." He explained the situation. "Can you do what's necessary to clear it with the boss?"

"Sure, that shouldn't be a problem. Where are you heading?"

"Virginia, to my grandparents' old home." Dave rubbed his chin. "It's not going to be fun driving there in the snow, but my truck has snow tires, so I don't think it will be too much of a problem. It's too late to leave now and we've been out celebrating our engagement, so it will be safer if we head out first thing in the morning."

"Congratulations! I'll clear it with everyone. Take your com and stay in contact. I react faster than the local cops if there are any concerns." Terabyte cleared his throat. *"You don't sound too worried."*

Dave shrugged as he pushed the buttons inside the elevator. "I'm not. She goes AWOL all the time, and if she'd been in an accident, the cops would have called me. I'm down as her next of kin. Josie often takes off for days. She turns off her phone when she doesn't want to be disturbed. I couldn't reach her for a full week one time. She considers cellphones an invasion of privacy. This is the problem with geniuses; they live in their world of academia and forget we all live on the outside."

"Okay, I'm here if you need me."

Dave thought for a minute. He'd broken protocol one time when Terabyte went missing for days and asked after his health on his return. He'd discovered his handler's wife had died, leaving him with three kids to raise. That's all the information he had about him but as Terabyte knew what he ate for breakfast, knowing this small part of his handler's life wasn't going to cause a national security breach. "Hey, how are things at home now? Are you coping okay with the kids?"

"Yeah, I'm working hard to keep sane. My ma helps with the kids. I'll never get over losing my wife but I'm taking it one day at a time. It's all we can do, right?"

Swallowing the lump in his throat, Dave slid one arm around Annie and stepped from the elevator. "Yeah. One day at a time." He disconnected.

CHAPTER TWENTY-THREE

It was close to eleven by the time Dave arrived in Virginia on Saturday morning. With Annie to keep him company even the snow hadn't spoiled the drive through the picturesque towns. It would be a good opportunity for him to introduce Annie to his last remaining family member. Although for all he knew, Josie could have driven home last night. He'd called his sister numerous times with no luck and left messages to ask her to call him. Problem was, she hated him checking up on her, and he'd probably receive the usual eyeroll and lecture she gave him about being capable of looking after herself. Even without taking a call, she should have checked her messages by now. Something didn't feel right and if he disturbed her tranquility, it was just too bad. He never ignored his gut feeling and it had saved his life many a time. He glanced at Annie as they turned onto the long road that led to the old house. Snow had fallen overnight, turning the surrounding landscape into a picture worthy of a Christmas card. It sure was beautiful out here. "That's the old place up ahead."

He drove through the open gate and spotted the pile of wood covered with snow. Ahead, the garage doors stood open to the weather and snowflakes dusted his sister's blue SUV. Relieved to see she hadn't left already, he drove in and parked beside it. "Well, it looks like she's here."

"Is she tall like you?" Annie pulled on her gloves.

Dave shook his head. "Nope, she's more like you. Small and blonde. My mom had Swedish parents. She was tall and fair but her father was my size. I figure the genes missed a female generation with Josie. My dad was much like me, dark hair, blue eyes."

"Was he as big as you?" Annie smiled at him.

"No, about six feet." He laughed. "I take after my grandfather in everything but hair color. I have his eyes and physique. Like him, I was this size at fourteen, so I never had a problem with bullies at school."

"Well, you know my dad is over six feet, so maybe our sons will be like you. I hope so." Annie squeezed his arm and giggled. "Although, if we're making wishes, I hope the girls take after me."

Dave cupped her cheek and kissed her. "I'll be happy no matter who they take after." He shook his head, so incredibly happy he choked up. "I can't believe I found you again and you want to marry me. In my line of work, I never thought I deserved a chance of happiness… it's like an incredible dream."

"It's real." Annie hugged him. "I'm real and I'm not going anywhere. It's no dream. It's happening on Monday at my parents' house at two."

Laughing, Dave hugged her. "We haven't even decided where to live. My place is bigger."

"Fine by me. I'd live in a lean-to with you. Just promise me one thing?" Annie gave him a determined stare. "Not even POTUS can stand in our way. I mean, how long can it take? The world can wait for an hour. It's about time you came first for a change."

Dave touched her flushed cheek. "I promise and I never break my word—not ever."

Reluctantly, he slid from behind the wheel. Each second with her was a gift. He hated leaving her and had requested two days compassionate leave so they could at least have a short honeymoon. Terabyte had worked his usual magic and pulled in a few favors, and now he didn't have to report until the following Friday. Annie too had found a legal temp to replace her for the week, so everything was set. There could be no turning back now.

Dave took her hand and they trudged through the thick snow to the front of the house. Lights were ablaze inside and as they climbed the front steps the door hanging open stopped him in his tracks. Someone had broken the lock. Leaves and melted snow covered the polished wooden floor. His stomach tightened. "Get behind me." He pulled his weapon and they eased inside the door. After listening to the clock ticking for some moments, Dave moved down the hallway. He raised his voice. "Josie, where are you? It's Junior. Josie, call out. Where are you?"

Nothing.

The old clock ticked and then with a whirring sound it chimed the hour. The eleven gongs echoed through the silent house. Dave pulled his backup pistol from his ankle holster and handed it to Annie. He backed her into the mudroom. "Someone's broken into the house. I'm going to clear this floor. Stay here, keep your back to the wall, and watch the stairs. If you see any movement, call out. If anyone comes at you, shoot them. Don't hesitate."

"Go, I'll be fine." Annie chambered a bullet and gave him a determined nod.

After dropping into his calm, fully alert mode, Dave cleared the ground floor. He eased into the kitchen and stared at the obvious sign of a struggle. It was cold inside, the back door wide open. Pots, pans, and knives littered the floor alongside a mobile phone in pieces, and blood spatter covered one wall, but not enough to suggest a kill. *Where are you, Josie?* He switched on his power pack and touched his com. "Terabyte, do you copy?"

"Copy."

Swallowing the dread crawling up his spine, Dave used his professional calm to evaluate the situation. "I'm at my grandparents' house." He explained the situation. "I'm going to clear the upper floor. Get the local boys out as backup."

"I'm on it."

Dave hurried back and nodded to Annie. "Stay there. I'll check upstairs."

"Have you found her?" Annie's weapon remained steady, her eyes darting back and forth.

Taking the steps two at a time, he reached the landing and paused. "Not yet."

Easing along the wall, he opened each door and checked inside. The room Josie had been using had an open suitcase on a chair. She hadn't unpacked. He hustled back down the stairs and went to Annie. "There are signs of a fight in the kitchen and the back door is open. The cops are on the way, but I'll need to go around the outside of the house. There's blood in the kitchen. It looks like someone was hurt and maybe ran out the door."

"Oh, my God!" Annie gripped his arm. "Do you think..."

Dread dropped over Dave like a shroud. His gut knotted. He'd trained his sister to defend herself and she was good. Whoever had broken in wouldn't have expected someone to fight back. The lights burning all through the house would suggest someone broke in Thursday or maybe Friday night. If Josie was okay, she'd have returned to the house by now. He gathered his thoughts. If something bad had happened, he'd need his professional calm to deal with it because, as sure as hell, without it he'd go ballistic.

He took Annie's hand and led her outside. "It doesn't look good. Stay close and walk in my footprints. Don't remove your gloves. Keep looking around. We'll be exposed outside for anyone hiding in the woods or barn. Josie must be here somewhere. It looks like she put up one hell of a fight and could be hiding in the barn." He led the way around the outside of the house. "Her phone is smashed, so she couldn't call for help."

"What was that?" Annie pressed closer.

Dave froze on the spot. A slow moaning sound followed by a thud came from close by. "Get behind me, close to the wall."

Scanning the building, searching back and forth, he stiffened when the sound came again. *Grind. Scrape, Thunk.*

"Where is it coming from?" Annie looked at him wide-eyed, her teeth chattering from the cold.

Dave dropped his voice to just above a whisper. "The house. Move slowly. Try not to make a sound."

They edged along the wall.

Grind. Scrape. Thunk.

He peeked around the corner and looked up. A window shutter was blowing in the wind, slowly opening before banging shut again. He looked at her. "It's just a shutter. Come on, we'll check the barn."

"Shouldn't we wait for the cops?" Annie tugged at his hand. "What if someone is still here?" She looked up at him and shook her head. "Okay, *I know.* One or ten, you'll deal with them, but you're not wearing Kevlar right now, so be careful, okay?"

Dave squeezed her hand. "Careful is my middle name."

CHAPTER TWENTY-FOUR

Scanning all around the house with every step through the deep snow, Dave moved slowly, keeping close to the outside of the house. The old barn would be the best place for Josie to hide. The root cellar had stored many things, including his grandfather's homemade wine collection and his grandmother's preserves. He remembered the smell of the sacks of potatoes on pallets against the wall and the skins falling down from the big brown onions hanging in strings from the rafters. As the building came into view, memories of visiting on holiday weekends filtered into his mind. It was usually his job to go down into the cellar to retrieve any items his grandparents needed. Usually, a bottle of wine for dinner, or a quantity of potatoes. The place gave him the creeps. Even on a sunny day, the old barn creaked and moaned with the slightest puff of wind, and going into the root cellar and down the steps in the dark was an absolute nightmare.

Although he'd never admitted it to his parents, just walking into the barn set his nerves on edge, as if his early gut feeling was issuing a warning to run for the hills. At eight years old, he had to jump to reach the cord attached to the light at the bottom of the steps, which meant walking into pitch black. The normal number of critters lived down there and scattered away from the light. Cobwebs seemed to grow like ivy and hung down all over. It never ceased to amaze him how, even as he'd grown, the idea of walking into that particular cellar spooked him. Now for once he had a reason.

After looking all around, they dashed across the space between the house and barn, stopping at the entrance with their backs against the wall. Dave turkey-peeked inside and the hairs on the back of his neck rose at the sight of the open cellar door hatch. It was always closed unless someone was down there. Although, it could be bolted on the inside. A precaution, he figured if used as a storm shelter. If Josie had hidden there, she would have slid the bolt across to protect herself. He scanned the loft and bent down to peer under the old tractor, but apart from the wind and snow blowing inside, there was no movement.

"How long will it take for the cops to arrive?" Annie squeezed his fingers.

Dave led her inside the barn. "Maybe half an hour, maybe more. The station is miles away and, with the snow and all, it will take some time." He stared at the open cellar hatch and back to Annie. "Get behind the tractor and keep watch. I'll go into the cellar." Unable to contemplate what he might find down there, he stared into her eyes. "I'll need you to watch my back."

"Okay." Annie moved into position. "Go, I'll be fine."

Dave pulled out his phone and accessed the flashlight. He moved toward the cellar, noting the small spatter of blood droplets on the cement floor. As he reached the hatch, he could plainly see someone had forced it open. A crowbar lay discarded close by. He shone the light down the steps and into the gaping black maw. All his old childhood fears ran at him like ghouls in the night determined to swallow him up with dread. He squared his shoulders. He'd faced death so many times, been confronted by impossible situations, and killed on command without fear clouding his judgement. He drew in a few deep breaths, watching the stream of steam from his mouth on the exhale, and dropped into the zone. His pounding heart slowed and everything came into sharp focus. This was his safe place, nothing bothered him, no emotions disturbed his thoughts. His control and resolve were unbreakable.

He pressed his com and started the video recorder on his phone. Dropping his voice to a whisper, he explained the situation to Terabyte and then started down the steps, avoiding the drips of blood. In one hand he held his Glock, in the other his phone. The string for the light came into view. It hung dirty and limp, covered in cobwebs. He tugged it and a dusty old light bulb flickered and went out. As he ducked under a low beam at the entrance, the stench of death slammed into him. Moving the light with slow deliberation he searched the floor and the light reflected in a large pool of blood. He gritted his teeth and moved closer as the legs of a body came into view. It was Josie, he recognized her snakeskin boots and froze midstride. His light moved over the spill of blonde hair, matted with crimson. There was so much blood. Her beautiful eyes had fixed in a death stare. Her face so pale and lips blue she was hardly recognizable as the vibrant woman he knew and loved. His defenses slid away and with his emotions naked, grief made him stagger. He slumped against the wall, unable to rationalize what had happened.

Minutes ticked by. The chilled air brushed his cheek, cooling the hot tears that he'd shed without noticing. A remoteness engulfed him in an out-of-body experience. As if he were seeing everything through a stranger's eyes. He couldn't be here, witnessing his sister's murder scene. Fate couldn't do that to him, could it? He reached for the zone again. Being out of control wasn't an option. He gave himself a mental shake and held the phone steady, recording the scene as if Josie were a stranger. After holstering his weapon, he touched his com. "Terabyte, do you copy?"

"Copy."

Dave straightened. He had to push his emotions to one side and, as first on scene, had to make a coherent detailed report. "I've found her. She's dead. Her throat's cut, multiple stab wounds. There are footprints all over and one of the kitchen knives from the house is on scene. I'll send you the video file now." He sent the file.

"Get out of there now. That's an order. I'll contact the cops again and tell them what's happened. Where's Annie? She's your priority now. The killer could still be on scene."

Dave moved the phone all around shedding light in every corner. "There's no one here and she's armed. I'm collecting evidence. This is a homicide."

"Snap out of it and do as I say. You're walking out of there right now." Terabyte raised his voice. *"You can't be involved in the investigation. Turn around, go back, and protect Annie. Do it now."*

"On my way." Dave stepped around the blood. He crouched down beside Josie and allowed his feelings to come back in a landslide of grief. He touched her ice-cold skin and closed her eyes. "I'll find out who did this to you, Sis, and make them pay." He stood and, with care not to contaminate the scene, walked out of the cellar forever.

CHAPTER TWENTY-FIVE

Washington, DC

Six months later

Annie sat at her desk in the reception area of the magistrate's office. It had been a quiet afternoon. Her boss was in court and she had time to reflect. The last six months had been an emotional roller coaster, to say the least. Although Dave was an expert at hiding his feelings, he'd been working through a range of emotions since his sister's murder. Of course, he blamed himself, even though the medical examiner had insisted she'd died on the Thursday night before the dean had contacted him. A neighbor had identified her killer as a man who'd called by earlier to collect wood from the old tree, only to return later to attack her. The murder had nothing to do with Dave's work. The serial killer had been murdering women all over the state. Josie had fought hard to protect herself and stabbed her attacker before running for the barn. The investigation hadn't taken very long at all. With friends in high places handling the case, it wasn't long before DNA and fingerprint databanks gave up the identity of her killer. Within a few days of her murder, the man was arrested and currently sat in jail awaiting his trial.

Annie glanced at the photograph of her wedding day and smiled. Dave insisted on wearing his sunglasses and a hat for the picture she'd wanted to display on her desk and they'd produced all the others on her father's office printer. Although grief stricken, Dave had insisted on the wedding going ahead as planned. They'd spent an entire week secluded in his apartment trying to block out the world before returning to work as Mr. and Mrs. Parkes. She had to smother a laugh when her magistrate boss had asked her straight out if Dave and her were related. She hadn't explained. She couldn't and just told him she'd been as amazed as him when she'd discovered her husband's last name.

The last couple of weeks Dave had been busy. There'd been two terrorist bombings in DC, resulting in the deaths of government employees, and it was all hands on deck trying to discover who was responsible. After working long hours, Dave arrived home exhausted but always had a smile for her. He'd proved to be a very caring and attentive husband. At work, flowers would arrive out of the blue, with little messages that made her smile. She'd never felt so loved. He was her everything.

The annoying sniff of the man who'd refused to leave the previous three days in a row brought her out of her daydream. As he walked toward her desk, she moved her chair backward. She'd spoken to Dave at length about him and had taken his advice to be distant and professional. "Can I help you?"

"Yeah, you can help me." The man placed his knuckles on her desk and glared at her. "I want an appointment to see the magistrate."

Annie drew a deep breath. "As I told you before, you'll need to speak to your lawyer. The magistrate deals with cases in court not in his office. He can't assist you with your case."

"Look, lady, I only want to ask him one simple question. One." He straightened and rocked back on his heels. "Can you at least ask him?"

Annie glanced at the clock. It was a little after three. "He should be back by five. When he gets out of court, I'll go and ask him personally and see if he can spare you a minute, but I know what his answer will be. He won't see you."

"I'll wait." The man sat down, folded his arms, and stared at her.

The hairs on the back of her neck prickled. She pulled out her phone and sent a text message to Dave, telling him the creepy guy was back. Seconds later, her phone buzzed and she sighed with relief at seeing his name on the caller ID. "Hey."

"Hey, you. I'll swing by just after five and give you a ride home. You can leave your SUV at work. I'll drop you at work in the morning. Problem solved. Creepy Guy won't hang around long once I arrive and politely ask him to leave."

Annie giggled. "Thanks, I'll see you soon." She disconnected and went back to work ignoring the man.

The annoying man had left by three-thirty and, relieved, Annie had worked on her files, various appointments, and other things scheduled for the magistrate. It had been close to five when Creepy Guy showed up again, carrying a backpack and a to-go cup of coffee. When he sat down and smiled at her, her stomach gave a sudden twist of alarm. Why was he being so nice?

The magistrate entered his chambers via a back door. He never came through the front office. When her phone buzzed, she picked up and listened. She glanced at Creepy Guy. She would ask her boss to see him but she already knew his answer. "I'll be right in."

She went inside and listened to the magistrate's instructions. It took some time to take down notes for the files he'd require for the next day. When he'd finished, she explained about the creepy man. "He won't give up. I tell him it's nothing to do with you but he won't listen to reason. This is the fourth day in a row I've refused to allow him to see you."

"I'm not seeing him. It would compromise my position. Send him on his way. If he shows up tomorrow, call security and have him removed." The magistrate smiled at her. "This sort of thing happens all the time. You'll get used to it. I'm heading home now and suggest you do the same."

Annie nodded and returned to her office, surprised to find it empty. She tidied her desk and looked up as Dave walked in the door, with a face like granite. She grinned at him and picked up her purse. "It looks like Mr. Creepy has left the building."

"That's good." Dave swept her into his arms and kissed her soundly. "How are you feeling?"

Annie grinned at him. "Wonderful but I have a hankering for Black Forest cake."

"Then we'll go home and change and I'll take you to dinner. I'm yours for the entire evening." Dave hugged her close. "Come on, my truck is waiting right out front."

CHAPTER TWENTY-SIX

The sun was dropping low in the sky as they left the building but it had been a beautiful day. It had been good to be outside for a time, although visiting the aftermath of a terrorist bombing had been harrowing. The powers that be had scrambled everyone, and hunting down who was targeting high-ranking government employees was a priority. The problem was, the usual terrorist organizations hadn't claimed responsibility, which had left everyone scratching their heads. With all the agencies working on the case, they'd still come up with zip. He'd been reassigned back to the White House, and some hotshot ex-navy Seal FBI bomb expert was taking the lead in the case.

He took Annie's hand as he walked down the steps. The last rays of sunshine lit up her hair making it look like spun gold. Every time he looked at her, he thanked God for giving him such a gift. He'd never been so happy. It was as if he'd found the missing part of his soul. They linked fingers as they walked to his truck. He leaned close to her ear. "I love you."

"I love you too." Annie's smile was brilliant.

He opened the truck door for her and waited for her to tuck her large purse under her legs, then walked around the hood and strapped in. The next second an explosion rocked the truck. Pain shot through his head as shattered windows sprayed glass all around him. He couldn't breathe or see through the thick smoke. He could hear people screaming and the truck's alarm was blaring. His body refused to move. Blood ran down his face and into one eye, dripping off his chin. In agony and trembling uncontrollably, he forced his throbbing head to turn an inch to search for Annie. As he looked at her beautiful face, something inside him died. She'd taken the full force of the bomb. He opened his mouth to scream but nothing came out. Fire was licking the seat around her but he couldn't move. He'd burn to death but he didn't care. Without Annie, his life was meaningless.

*

Dave didn't like the lights in his eyes. He batted them away, wondering why the afterlife was so damn annoying. His head ached, and his mouth was so dry his tongue stuck to the roof. In fact, everything hurt. Well, no wonder he'd ended up in hell. He figured he kind of deserved it. His mind went to Annie and a pain hit his heart and made him gasp. If he were in hell, he'd never see her again. He choked back a sob as his last memory of her slammed into his mind. Not the smiling happy face that had been with him since Syria but her death mask. Oh yeah, he'd gone straight to purgatory and this was part of his punishment.

"Ninety-eight H." The voice wasn't anyone he recalled. "Open your eyes."

Dave cracked open his lids and as his vision cleared, he stared at a man in uniform. He didn't recognize him but a quick scan of the room told him it was a hospital. Machinery beeped and he had wires attached everywhere.

"You're in Maryland at the Walter Reed National Military Medical Center." The man offered him a drink from a cup with a bent straw. "I'm Captain Murray, the doctor assigned to your recovery."

Dave drank until the doctor dragged the cup away. He looked at him. "My wife?"

"I'm sorry, she didn't make it." The doctor laid a hand on his shoulder. "She died instantly if it's of any comfort to you."

"Comfort? Someone killed my wife. I need to be there making sure they treat her right. Get these wires off me." Anger rolled off him. He wanted to punch something. The machines started going nuts and Murray pulled a syringe from a drawer. Dave glared at him. "Don't stick me with anything, or I'll break your neck."

"I'll call for help if you don't calm down." Murray's expression filled with compassion. "I know what you are and your unique abilities. Use them now to control your anger. Pushing your blood pressure too high at this stage of recovery could cause a stroke."

"I don't know what you're talking about." Dave glared at him. "We've never met." With effort, he smothered the grief threatening to destroy him. The military wouldn't give him time to mourn his wife, so for now he'd become the machine they'd created. He dropped so deep into the zone that his low heart rate set off a warning on the monitor.

"I've never seen that before. That's impressive. I have clearance, so you can speak freely with me." Murray had taken a step back, his fingers still clinging to a loaded syringe.

Dave frowned. "Do you now, Captain. Then you'll know, I only speak to Terabyte. What time is it?"

"Midday." The doctor dropped the needle on a tray and adjusted the drips running into him. "It's November 7th. You've been in an induced coma for four months."

Astonished, Dave blinked. "Explain."

"The blast sent a piece of metal into your skull. In simple terms, we had to repair it with a metal plate. There was substantial brain swelling and we had to wait for it to subside. You're not out of the woods yet. The fact you are coherent and speaking is a good sign but you may have to learn to walk again and even feed yourself. You have a long and hard road ahead of you, I'm afraid."

Dave wiggled his toes and moved his legs. He touched his nose with each index finger and tried to sit up. Pain slammed through his head in waves of agony. Nausea hit him and he flopped back, gagging. After he gathered himself, he looked at Murray. "Seems to me everything is working fine apart from my head."

"I'll give you something for the nausea and then I'll sit you up." Murray pushed a needle into the drip line. "Seeing you move so well after lying so long flat on your back is a very positive sign. Unfortunately, the plate in your head will cause headaches and these will lessen as time goes by, but at first, like now, when you move you will experience, pain, dizzy spells, and nausea, which we can treat with drugs." He smiled. "It's really up to you now."

As the back of the bed rose slowly, Dave gingerly touched his head. No bandages but he could feel how short they'd cut his hair, although it had grown back some over a lumpy scar over one ear. He looked at the doctor. "I need to speak to Terabyte. Can you arrange that?"

"Do you remember his number?" The doctor pulled a phone in a sealed box out of the drawer. He broke the seal and handed it to him. "I was instructed to do this in front of you."

"Yeah, my memory is fine." His stomach rumbled and he looked at the doctor. "Can I get something to eat?" He examined his arms and peered under the sheet. He'd lost half of his body mass. "I need protein."

"Maybe some Jell-O to start." Murray smiled. "Slow and easy is the best way to go." He turned and left the room.

Dave punched in Terabyte's number. It was good to hear his voice. He gave his code name and waited for a reply. The verification came through and the line secure. "I lost Annie. Have you found the bomber?"

"You sound lucid. How long since you woke up?"

Annoyed, Dave let out a long sigh. "Just before and my brain is working overtime. My body is a mess but I'll be fine. Did you catch the damn bomber?"

"We have everyone on it. There are a few leads and I'll update you as they eventuate." Terabyte sighed. *"I'm really sorry about Annie."*

Dave pulled out the drip to the saline and dropped it on the floor. The morphine he'd leave for just a bit longer. He needed to talk about Annie but his chest hurt so bad he couldn't get the words out. After taking a few deep breaths, he composed himself. "Where is she?"

"Her father took care of everything. She is buried in the family plot beside you."

Dave swallowed hard, thinking he'd misheard him. "Say again?"

"You heard me right. You're officially dead. I went to the funeral and took a video. I know it sounds morbid but I figured you would've wanted to be there and this is the next best thing." Terabyte paused a beat. *"I know what pain you're going through and it doesn't get better but we can live with it. They say time heals, so put any ideas of self-harm out of your mind. It isn't a solution. One day at a time is our motto, right?"*

The pain at losing Annie was stuck just above his heart. He'd never forget her. He didn't want to and would always remember their time together and the love they shared. Dave nodded and regretted it immediately. "Yeah, Annie wouldn't like me to eat a bullet, so I guess you're stuck with me, but my future isn't so bright right now. A desk job at best, I figure."

"Nah, you're a valuable player, carrying national secrets. POTUS wants you protected and has planned a future for you. While you're out of commission, you'll get a new face, identity, and job if you want one, but not in DC."

Trying hard to focus, Dave rubbed his aching head. "I don't need a job or my old identity to access the funds in the offshore account. It's by a retina scanner via an app on my phone. If I still have a phone."

"All that is already in motion. POTUS's office will produce postdated documents to have everything in both your and Annie's estates, including life insurance policies, moved into your offshore company. Once

we establish your new identity, you'll have a bank account fed by the company and a regular paycheck from Uncle Sam. Everything will be organized for you."

Dave sighed. "I doubt I'll be in active service again, not with a plate in my head. Heck, right now I can't even walk to the john. Sitting up made me spew."

"Just get well and I'll start looking for a nice quiet place for you to retire."

"Hell no." Dave snorted. "No retiring. I'll go nuts. Can't I just go dark and hide in the mountains somewhere out west and become a lone vigilante fighting for justice?"

"I'll see what I can do." Terabyte's voice sounded amused. *"You'll need a new name. Anything come to mind?"*

Dave thought for a beat but it was obvious. "Dave was Annie's pet name for me. I'll use Dave, so Annie will be with me forever."

"Okay. That would work well because it's best to keep your original initials, so you don't accidentally sign your old name. What about Kane for the middle name? It means 'warrior.' If I recall, Annie called you her warrior." Terabyte's enthusiasm flowed through the speaker. *"What last name do you like?"*

After considering a few options, Dave sighed. "I figure, Dave Kane will suit me just fine. David Kane the Wild West vigilante."

"Hmm. I'll work on a background story. It will have to be close to your skill set. A detective from a major city perhaps and then you can mention a head injury… maybe shot in the head in the line of duty?" The sound of Terabyte typing came through the earpiece. *"There's heaps of work out west for deputies. When you're back on your feet, we'll discuss your options."*

The door opened and a woman pushing a cart came in his room. "Okay, I'll speak to you soon. My Jell-O has just arrived."

CHAPTER TWENTY-SEVEN

Walter Reed National Military Medical Center

Dave decided right from the start, he didn't cope well in rehab. First up, he'd lost his balance and standing made him nauseous. In fact, just turning his head made him want to spew. It had been a nightmare and one it seemed hadn't fully abated. He'd bend and pain would cripple him and it would start all over again. The head didn't have the only injuries. The blast had broken ribs and chipped one hip, but they'd healed during the coma. He'd lost half his bodyweight and he missed his muscle strength. His brain kept telling him he'd turned into a weakling, to give up as life wasn't worth living anyway. Depression had him by the throat and he'd stare at the ceiling for hours. He'd refused the drugs, taking only the ones for the severe headaches and nausea when absolutely necessary. Becoming an opiate junkie wasn't on his agenda.

Dragging heavy legs into the bathroom, he stared at the unfamiliar face in the bathroom mirror. The swelling from the plastic surgery had subsided. The scar on his chin and over one eye had gone. He had a straight nose, like when he was eighteen, and a dimple in his chin. They'd removed the ravages of long years spent out in the desert from his skin. Apart from his eyes, his own mother wouldn't have recognized him. His phone buzzed and he pulled it out of his pocket. Terabyte called him usually once a week on Fridays to check on him, and as it was Monday, something must be up. He pressed the phone to his ear. "Morning."

"I've just read the report from your doctor. In all the years I've been handling you, I've never known you to give up." Terabyte took a breath. *"You're not eating and you're way behind in your recovery. This isn't good because I've found a potentially perfect job for you."* He sighed. *"But if you've given up, we'll send someone else. But this young woman needs someone with your skill set and compassion."*

Dave stared at his reflection. He'd shrunk into a person he didn't recognize. Sure, he had the six-five height but he resembled a stick insect. "Give me a break. Have you forgotten what I do, or should I say *did*, before the bombing? My mindset hasn't changed. I kill people on demand with no remorse. I might as well be a serial killer. I don't have compassion."

"Says the man who put his life on the line to save Annie."

A wave of loss smacked into him and he straightened. His father had raised him to hide his feelings and his Marine training had obliterated them. Not feeling was part of survival. He gathered himself and walked back into the small room that had been his home for the last six months. "I'm not ready for a mission."

"It's not a mission."

Dave shook his head slowly, ignoring the constant headache. "Don't think giving me a woman to protect is going to replace Annie. You should know better."

"I'd never suggest such a thing and, as sure as hell, Jenna Alton doesn't need protecting. I can't give you details, other than the US Marshals are involved to some extent. There are rumors that the previous sheriff, let's say, overlooked crimes. People gone missing, bones found in Stanton Forest that he dismissed as Native American relics, women being abused—all came to light well before Sheriff Alton was elected. We figure there's more to Black Rock Falls than meets the eye. She's a smart cookie but with

few resources. Between the two of you, if anything illegal went down, you'd be able to work together to sort it. Together you'd be able to handle anything that might go down in the future. You know as well as I do these vast forests are perfect for criminals to hide off the grid. Anyone could be lurking in there."

Interest rose like a buoy thrown to a drowning man. He enjoyed fighting crime, and in a sleepy town what could be better? He flexed his sagging muscles and sighed. "I'm no good to anyone right now. I'm weak and I'll need time to recover."

"You have until winter. Later today, we're moving you into specialized rehab. Everything will be tailored to getting you back into shape. In ten months, you'll be better than before. You'll be taken to a range to shoot, and when you're not working out and eating, you'll be studying Montana law and anything else we figure you'll need."

Dave pictured the Big Sky Country and it was as if someone had opened a magic portal of hope. He stared out the window, imagining the mountains, rivers, and tall pines. "In case it slipped your mind, I still have a bounty on my head. New face maybe, but terrorist organizations can hack anything. My prints and retina scan can't be altered. I'll make the place more dangerous."

"We want you to keep a low profile but hiding you in plain sight is better. It works, even for those in witness protection. You'll be so off the grid, no one will believe it's you." Terabyte cleared his throat. *"POTUS knows, you'll recover and with assistance be better than you were before… well, apart from the metal plate. There's always a chance you'll be returned to active duty but he wants to give you time to recover in mind and body. You need time to grieve."*

Dave held out his arm. The shakes had subsided and his bulk would return if he ate enough protein and worked his butt off. In ten months, he'd be a machine. "Give me a profile of this woman who needs my help."

"Jenna Alton is strong-willed, feisty, and set in her ways. She has an old deputy by the name of Walters and maybe two rookies." He cleared his throat. *"She needs someone solid beside her but the last thing she needs to know is you're there to back her up. She'd likely take it as an insult, so keep that in mind when you meet her."*

The vision of the backwoods town still hung in his mind. No memories to haunt him, a new beginning, a new face and name. Maybe he could make it one step at a time. He sighed. "So, are you planning on sending me to take her job and run the show? That doesn't sound like keeping a low profile and it's not something I'm comfortable doing. I have a lot of respect for women as they often have to claw their way to the top. Sorry but this isn't my gig. I can't take charge of myself just yet, let alone a sheriff's department."

"You'll need time to adjust, we know that—I know that. We don't want you to take her job, just the opposite." Terabyte sighed. *"You don't have to decide now. In ten months, you'll be fit and we'll talk again, but it's the incentive you need, Dave. The advertisement for position of deputy sheriff has had no takers for six months and they took it down this week. We have a cover story for you as a gold shield detective, shot in the line of duty, looking for a place to recover. If you decide it's a go, we'll contact the sheriff's department and make sure you get the position."*

With his gut waving red flags at him, Dave shook his head. "I don't buy it. What's really going on here? What is it about Jenna Alton you're not telling me?"

"I've told you everything I can. She's not a born Montanan and had to make her stand in Black Rock Falls. She's fighting to prevent violence against women and won an election for a four-year term. We'd like to see her succeed. It's a big county with many undesirables and she needs someone like you to watch her back."

Dave scrubbed a hand through his short hair and sighed. "She'll look at me as a threat to her job."

"Then you make it clear from the get-go you're looking for a quiet life." Terabyte paused for some seconds as if thinking. *"It's the chance for a normal life, Dave. Fishing, hunting, camping in the forest. Peace."*

Could he leave? Annie would always be with him, no matter where he went. As sure as hell, he couldn't stay holed up in a hospital for the rest of his life. At the moment he had no purpose. He'd become weak in mind and spirit but had the willpower to change. He just had to get with the program and stop wallowing in self-pity. Nothing would bring his wife back. The only way was moving forward alone and he'd survived alone before just fine. He rested his forehead on the glass, allowing the sun to make rainbows in his tears. He could almost hear Annie's voice in his head, encouraging him. "Okay, I'll do it. One step at a time, right?"

"Yeah, Dave. One step at a time."

CHAPTER TWENTY-EIGHT

It was coming into winter as Dave strolled along the sidewalk, kicking at the leaves. A shiver of excitement went through him and the freezing wind had nothing to do with it. It was cold in Helena, Montana, and when an icy chill hit the metal plate in his head, the headaches would come in a rush. He'd worn double woolen caps and pulled up the hood on his jacket to keep warm but he'd need to acclimatize a little more before heading to Black Rock Falls. He'd recovered almost completely; the metal plate would always be a problem but his body was better than before, and now he hit the scales at two hundred and sixty-plus pounds of solid muscle. He hadn't lost his ability to shoot the wings off a fly and still never missed. He'd surprisingly returned to peak performance.

Over the past couple of months POTUS had forwarded him specifications of a high-performance truck, bombproof and with bulletproof glass. Tricked out with all the gadgets, it had a safe and gun locker built in and flashing lights set into the grill. It was a magnificent truck. The one thing Dave understood was engines. He could rebuild just about any engine by the time he hit sixteen and, being alone on missions, his skill had saved him many a time. He increased his pace. Up ahead he spotted the truck stop and scanned the parking lot for a blue fourteen-wheeler. The early morning ice cracked under his boots as he made his way over the gravel. He approached the truck and a man jumped down from the passenger side and headed toward him. Dave stood his ground, hands loose at his sides. If this was his delivery, it would be covered by a US Marshal or Secret Service. Without saying a word, he pulled out the paperwork and handed it to the man.

"Okay." The man handed the papers back and walked around the back of the truck, opened the doors, and dropped down ramps. "Stand back." He gave a hand signal to the driver.

A mechanical sound came from inside the truck and very slowly a massive black truck emerged, rolled down the ramps, and settled on the ground. It was bigger than Dave expected, and the paintwork had a protective coating that made it shine. He swallowed hard. It was his dream machine. He looked at the man. "Thanks. Where are the papers and keys?"

"It has smart keys. They're in the glovebox with the paperwork, plus I'm to give you this." He gave Dave an envelope. "We had one hell of a job getting it into the truck. It's a beast of a thing."

"Yeah." Dave smiled. "But it's my beast."

He waited for the fourteen-wheeler to leave and walked around his prize. He climbed inside, retrieved the keys, and looked over the registration. The interior smelled of leather and when he hit the start button, the engine roared into life. He allowed it to idle and opened the envelope. The letter was from Terabyte. Inside was an application for the deputy sheriff's job in Black Rock Falls. It was completed apart from his signature. He grinned. He had to post it. "Man, do they still post mail around here?"

The letter contained information for the combination to a safe hidden in the back of the truck. They'd used his father's birthday, same for a gun locker containing various weapons, his sniper rifle, and ammo. He could change the combination and add a thumbprint for security. The safe held $200,000, five passports in various identities, and six burner phones. His getaway package. After memorizing the information about Sheriff Alton and Black Rock Falls, he stepped out of the truck, and using a Zippo, burned the letter in a nearby garbage bin.

It was all set. He had his vehicle, the job would come through in a couple of weeks, his wallet held a card to a virtually bottomless bank account, and now he had the Beast. Yeah, a good name for his truck. He climbed back in and took the brute for a run. It was easier to handle than he imagined and he headed out on the highway. The Beast was well named and roared with power. Driving it make him feel as if he were flying a jet. After an hour of excitement, he reluctantly headed back to his hotel.

After reading through the application, he added his phone number and email address, saying he was traveling. His cover story was set in place and he'd memorized it without a problem, even making sure he knew all the little things about his former workplace he should know on the off chance someone might question him. He understood Sheriff Jenna Alton would check out his creds and then decide if she wanted him on her team. After so long with no applications for the deputy sheriff's job, it should be a slam dunk. His cover letter mentioned he'd seen the advertisement some time ago and queried if the position was still available. His stomach rumbled and he checked his watch. The local diner would be open for breakfast and he planned to eat everything on the menu and then find a mailbox and post his letter. As he headed downstairs, his phone chimed. The only person who had his number was Terabyte. "Morning."

"I recall your interest in profiling and criminal behavior. It was in your field of study and I added it to your list of qualifications on the job application."

Dave smiled. "Yeah, so I see, not that I'll need it in Black Rock Falls." He chuckled. "Unless I need to profile a cattle rustler."

"That's beside the point." Terabyte took a breath. *"Every few years they have a law enforcement conference in Helena, with speakers on the*

criminal mind and various advances in technology. It's next weekend. I thought maybe you'd like to go."

Dave headed out of the hotel and hustled along the sidewalk toward the smell of the diner. "I'm not currently in law enforcement, and how would I obtain a ticket at this late date?"

"Why can't I ever get a straight answer from you? Do you want to go, yes or no?"

Stepping around a woman being pulled along by two massive dogs, Dave grinned. "I'd love to attend."

"Good. Pick up your tickets at the door. I'll send you the details." He disconnected.

Dave spent his time exploring Helena and giving the Beast a daily workout. The first snow came in a rush of white. The air was so clean and fresh it made him want to forget the idea of becoming a deputy and just stay in Helena, but he had his orders. After hearing the weather forecast, he decided to fit his truck with snow tires. When the offer of a job came through, he'd need to carry supplies in the snow for the trip to Black Rock Falls. The town wasn't at all small but it was remote. The county's long border ran alongside two other counties and even getting to the outskirts of Black Rock Falls would be a long arduous trip, with nothing in between the smattering of towns. He made a list of things he'd need: fuel, water, spare tires, and food. His clothing was reasonable but as the temperatures dropped daily, he headed for the local supply store for extra boots, jeans, jackets, and thermal underwear.

On his return, from an early breakfast, he filled his thermos with coffee at the diner and headed back to his room. The hotel offered food but not in the quantities or quality he required. The diner catered to truckers and offered the portion sizes he preferred. He placed the thermos on a small desk, sat down, and opened his laptop. The email logo flashed and he smiled at the official letter. It was confirmation of the deputy sheriff's job. His salary was more than reasonable for doing practically nothing, and an offer of housing if necessary. They supplied everything, apart from a weapon. He composed a reply and shot it back saying he'd be heading their way.

In a few minutes, the cheerful welcoming email from Deputy Rowley arrived with the GPS coordinates for the Black Rock Falls Sheriff's Office. Dave stared at the page wondering why the sheriff hadn't replied to him personally. He shrugged. There couldn't be an outbreak of crime in such a backwoods town, although from the map, the county encompassed a million square acres, most of it comprised of Stanton Forest and the Black Rock mountain range. The falls, from what he could see from the images on the internet, consisted of the vast Black Rock Falls and various smaller falls all of which ran into rivers and lakes throughout the county and beyond. The two neighboring towns were Louan to the north and Blackwater to the south. The county of Black Rock Falls, although isolated, had working mines, timber mills, and a meat-processing plant, all set in a massive and diverse industrial area in the lowlands. The main township was fast becoming a tourist destination, especially during the many festivals.

He read with interest about the art exhibitions in the town hall. The local hockey team had won the finals the previous year. The town appeared to have an endless supply of surprises. The images of the school and a college campus intrigued him, especially with the diversity of studies available. It seemed the "small, backwoods" town Terabyte had selected for him to "retire" was a huge diamond in the rough. He rubbed his chin, perusing the images of the main street: wide with a ton of stores and a park for kids that took up a good space on one side, banks, a turf-and-surf eatery, and a cute diner by the name of Aunt Betty's Café. He smiled to himself. *Gotta love that.*

After checking out the local accommodation, he found a motel on the outskirts of town, and, from the tariff, what looked like an upscale hotel. He made a note of the phone number. It was winter and he doubted he'd have any problems getting a room at The Cattleman's Hotel on arrival. He'd stay there until he found himself a place to live. He'd prefer to choose a place himself, away from other folks. Out of town maybe. He wasn't a social animal. From the local real estate listings, he'd have a choice of many rental properties. He stood and packed his overnight bag. The Beast was out front and ready to go.

After checking out, he headed out to his truck, placed the thermos into the console, and made sure everything he needed was at hand. He turned on the radio to catch the latest road report, punched his destination into the GPS, and eased the Beast into the flow of traffic. The time alone had been relaxing. Being in Montana and feeling the unrestricted freedom of space had eased his pain. He'd take the future one day at a time because he knew his wife would always be with him, locked in his heart. As he headed for the highway, all around him was a sea of snow. It was beautiful. He smiled. "Well, Annie, here I go to start a new life. Stay close. I figure I'm going to need an angel on my shoulder."

EPILOGUE

Washington, DC

Now

Dave Kane wiped away a tear running unashamedly down his cheek, the emotion he'd kept deep inside spilling out as he adjusted the potted rosebush he'd laid on Annie's grave. Red rose petals spilled over the grass mound like confetti as he straightened and placed one hand on the ice-cold marble headstone. Always on alert, Wolfe had waited some ways away as he'd crouched down and told Annie about his new life, about Jenna, and his plans for the future. It was something he needed to do, although achieving it had been a security nightmare. One hint of him being alive and he'd be hunted down and killed. Ninety-eight H might be officially dead, but terrorists had eyes everywhere and had access to technology that could break his cover.

As the cold wind brushed his cheek and the fall leaves rolled across the lawn, he recalled the day he'd married Annie. It had been a time filled with great joy and terrible sadness. His sister's murder had rocked him to the core, but Annie had been his strength and he'd promised her they'd marry and he never broke his word. She'd healed his grief and given him purpose. Their life together had been the fairy tale he'd never imagined possible, but he'd lost her. He'd been alone for too long, and had to move forward. He'd risked everything to visit her grave but it was worth it. Of course, he'd always imagined he'd be the first to die and the thought of Annie living alone for the rest of her life had troubled him. His heart ached as he remembered kissing the wedding band after slipping it on her finger and asking for her promise to find another if he died, only to have her do the same. The vision of her glowing face that day filled his head with a beautiful memory and replaced the death mask that had haunted him for so long. She'd always be with him, locked inside his heart, but it was time to keep his promise to her and move on. He traced her name on the stone and swallowed the lump in his throat. "Goodbye, Annie."

As he walked away, the sun broke through the clouds and a wide blue sky opened up as if guiding him home to Black Rock Falls, and the future awaiting him.

A LETTER FROM D.K. HOOD

Thank you so much for choosing my novel and coming back in time with me so I could tell you David Kane's story in *Lose Your Breath.*

If you loved this book and would like to stay up to date with all of my new releases, sign up here for my mailing list. You can unsubscribe at any time and your details will never be shared.

www.bookouture.com/dk-hood

It was very emotional for me to write a backstory that has resided inside my head for twelve books. I hope now you'll understand the reason Kane is such a complicated man, who can change between warm and compassionate to combat mode in a split second. I must admit I haven't told you everything about Dave Kane and there will be more secrets to reveal as the series unfolds.

If you enjoyed my story, I would be very grateful if you could leave a review and recommend my book to your friends and family. I really love hearing from readers, so feel free to ask me questions at any time. You can get in touch on my Facebook page or Twitter or through my blog.

Thank you so much for your support.
D.K. Hood

ACKNOWLEDGEMENTS

Thank you to my husband, Gary, for the encouragement and copious boxes of tissues I needed to write this story. His tireless assistance during the enormous amount of research I completed was priceless. Also, a huge call-out to the amazing #TeamBookouture for giving me the chance to tell you Dave Kane's unique story.

CPSIA information can be obtained
at www.ICGtesting.com
Printed in the USA
LVHW090055251121
704426LV00004B/588